THE MYSTERY OF RUBY'S TRACKS

ROSE DONOVAN

Moon Snail Press

MORE RUBY DOVE MYSTERIES

Join my reader group! Details can be found at the end of *The Mystery of Ruby's Tracks*.

Cast of Characters on Train Blanc[*]

Ruby Dove – Student of chemistry at Oxford, fashion designer, and amateur spy-sleuth. Thrilled to be returning home to Oxford after a rather eventful tour of Italy.

Fina Aubrey-Havelock – Student of history at Oxford. Ruby's assistant seamstress and best friend. Looking forward to their journey aboard the luxurious *Train Blanc*.

James Matua – First-year history student at Oxford. From New Zealand. A rather clumsy spy.

Pixley Hayford – A shameless journalist on the hunt for a scoop. Now good friends with Ruby and Fina.

Neeya Arafa – An accomplished student of the law. Lover of clothes but also possessor of little fashion sense.

Laurent Belrose – *Train Blanc* conductor. A good-humoured chap, but only if he's not pushed too far.

Etienne Durand – French diplomat with impeccable suits and impeccable timing.

Maurice Gaudin – Famous chef on *Train Blanc*. A curmudgeon with a nasty toothpick habit.

Ada Hartman – A plain-speaking German grandmother. Loves cards and knitting hideous scarves.

Raoul Lapointe – Sophia Salazar's personal secretary with a taste for the occult.

Julien Paquet – Earnest young *Train Blanc* attendant. Means to get ahead.

Sophia Salazar – Erotic writer and *femme fatale*.

Felix Schweinsteiger – A Swiss priest with a penchant for earthly delights.

Dorothy Synge – An irritable yet analytical young woman. Sister to Ridgewell.

Madeline Synge – A fan of Sophia Salazar's books. Mother to Dorothy and Ridgewell.

Ridgewell Synge – A quiet cove with an artistic bent. Brother to Dorothy.

Eustace Wistow – Former British colonial governor who wants to be the life of the party.

Ricki – Raoul's kitten. Has expensive tastes.

*Some characters have been omitted in order to maintain an element of surprise!

MAP OF TRAIN BLANC

Rear of the Train

Sleeping Carriage 1
    Cabin 12: *Pixley Hayford*
    Cabin 11: *Ruby Dove and Fina Aubrey-Havelock*
    Cabin 10: *James Matua*
    Cabin 9: *Neeya Arafa*
    Cabin 8: *Sophia Salazar*
    Cabin 7: *Raoul Lapointe*

Sleeping Carriage 2
    Cabin 6: *Ada Hartman*
    Cabin 5: *Etienne Durand*
    Cabin 4: *Dorothy and Madeline Synge*
    Cabin 3: *Ridgewell Synge*
    Cabin 2: *Governor Eustace Wistow*

Cabin 1: *Father Felix Schweinsteiger*

Lounge Carriage

Dining Carriage

Staff & Galley Carriage
   Galley
   Sleeping Berths: *Laurent Belrose, Julien Paquet, and Maurice Gaudin*

Engine

1

———

"Where did you hide the tickets?"

Fina looked at Ruby. Ruby glared at Pixley. Pixley held up his hands in mock surrender.

"I put them in my breast pocket," he said, wiping his bald-as-a-billiard-ball head. He stuck his stubby fingers in each pocket and wiggled them. "I swear I put them there as soon as you handed them to me at the hotel last night, Ruby."

Ruby Dove stood in her grey travelling outfit, arms crossed, feet tapping, and not a hair out of place. Despite the circumstances, Fina smiled at her best friend's impeccable sense of style and ability to stay so composed under pressure, no matter the season or place.

A man in a navy suit careened into Pixley Hayford, sending his briefcase flying onto the train platform, just a few inches from the edge. The briefcase spilt open. Sheaves of typing paper flew everywhere, merrily catching the breeze.

"No!" screeched Pixley. "My notes for the next three articles!" He crouched to retrieve the absconding paper. He didn't have far to bend over as he was only an inch or two taller than the diminutive Fina. Though he was stout, his blazer sleeves strained under pressure from his bulky muscles – so much so that they threatened to split open.

Ruby and Fina set down their suitcases and stamped on the paper flying around the platform.

"How rude," said Fina, glaring at the retreating back of the man in the fedora and expensively cut suit. He kept walking toward his destination as if nothing had happened.

"We're used to it." Ruby sighed.

Pixley nodded. "Or haven't you noticed?"

Fina didn't know how to respond to this obvious point so she grimaced in agreement. She cast her mind back to that restaurant incident in Milan. The owner had only let her in, turning away Pixley and Ruby once he saw the colour of their skin. Not that there hadn't been plenty of other moments of prejudice – this was just the most recent one.

"Should I hop down onto the track to catch those last few pieces?" groaned Pixley.

Ruby clamped a restraining hand on Pixley's arm.

"Absolutely not. I realise journalists are fanatical, but a story is not worth risking your life," she said, not unkindly.

"That's what you think," he said, sighing. "You're right, though. At least I typed up these notes on the Italian invasion of Ethiopia last night. I can remember most of it. I'll retype them when we're on the train."

"The train to Rome leaves in five minutes from platform five," boomed the loudspeaker in Italian.

"Train? We won't be on *Train Blanc* unless we find those tickets," said Fina, shivering. She pulled up the collar of her new tailored herringbone overcoat to the nape of her neck. The soft wool didn't scratch or tickle at all. And why should it? They had been shopping in Milan a few days before to prepare for this trip on *Train Blanc* – named for its route from Genoa through the snowy Alps to Lausanne. The final stop was Paris. Though Genoa was warm compared to England in November, a chill still ran through her. She must have become accustomed to the mild climate of Sardinia over the past few weeks.

She shook her head as she tried to push away memories of the island of Agrodoce. The best way to cope with trauma and tragedy – or at least the only way she had found to cope – was to keep moving and working. This strategy had carried her through several tragedies in the past two years. First, the murder of her father and the execution of her brother for the crime, then the murders: at Pauncefort Hall, on the *SS Sanguine*, back at Oxford, and then in Sardinia. Somehow, through it all, she and Ruby had remained friends and even become closer.

"Feens," said Ruby. "Are you there?" She tapped her watch. "The train is in thirty minutes. We must be on it."

Fina shook her head, though more in response to the unbearable cloud of perfume wafting from a passing woman than to her daydreams. She recognised the scent but couldn't remember the name. Her sensitive nose meant she avoided wearing perfume.

"It's *Nuit de Longchamp*," said Ruby, smiling at Fina. "In case you were wondering. It's lovely, isn't it?"

"A bit much for my taste," replied Fina as she watched the woman saunter in the same direction as the rude navy-suited man. Unlike everyone else about her, this woman walked at an unhurried pace. She wore a beautiful green wool crepe suit with chenille-embroidered horizontal lines – a design from that very year, if not the previous month. A close-fitting beret with a few tasteful green feathers perched at an angle on her head. A few steps behind her trundled a tall man in a garish burgundy suit. He held three suitcases under one arm and a dodgy box-contraption in another. Gasping, he said, "Sophia, darling, would you take Ricki? I'm afraid I'll drop everything unless I can rearrange this luggage."

"Train to Paris departs in twenty-five minutes from platform seven," scratched the loudspeaker.

"Surely there must be another train to Paris today," said Pixley, as he stuck his hands in his pockets and bounced up and down. Poor Pixley wasn't dressed for this inclement weather. And he had been unwilling to spend any money on an overcoat in Milan. He liked to say he was thrifty when it came to money. Fina was as well – because she didn't have any. But it had been worth spending this amount on a coat that would last for years to come in Oxford.

"There is another train today, but that's beside the point," said Ruby. "Ian told us we had to be on *Train Blanc* today – and in the cabins he chose for us. That's why he sent us the tickets."

"We haven't a bean between us," said Fina. "But what if we pool our money and purchase new tickets? We still have time." She squinted at the station clock. She swore the minute hand jumped five spaces as soon as she looked at it. Twenty minutes before the train left the station.

"For the *Train Blanc*? You must be joking," said Pixley. "It practically costs a year's salary for me." He pulled his trouser pockets inside-out to emphasise the point.

"Appears you three are between the devil and the deep blue sea, what?" squeaked a voice from behind them.

2

"James!" cried Fina. She spun around, nearly knocking him in the shins with her suitcase.

"Speak of the devil," said Pixley with a wry smile.

And there he was, the devil himself. Or the hand-maiden of the devil. James Matua: Oxford student, spy, and a generally irritating limpet. No, leech was a better description. The British government had ordered James to follow them wherever they went – in the first case to Sardinia and now, apparently, home to Oxford. They did not know if James was a willing spy, or if the authorities had forced him into the position under duress.

He stood there, grinning, as if meeting them was the best thing that had ever happened to him. But Fina couldn't watch his eyes, covered as they were by his floppy hair. Ruby had taught her to study people's eyes to avoid being led astray by more easily controlled facial expressions.

Ruby was having none of this. "What are you doing here? Are you following us? First, Sardinia. And then I could have sworn I spied you yesterday in Milan. And now this."

A little thrill of pride shot through Fina as she realised her own blunt style was rubbing off on Ruby.

James' mouth gaped open as wide as the sea. "I – I – I—" he stammered.

"I'm sorry, James. We have to catch a train, and we're already late," said Ruby, scooping up her suitcase.

"But you won't be able to catch your train without these," he said as he pulled from his pocket three train tickets. He displayed them as if he were a magician asking for a volunteer for his next trick.

Now it was Fina's turn to gape.

"Where did you find our tickets?" asked Ruby as she inspected them.

"Near the entrance to the station," he said. "I watched them fly out of Pixley's pocket when he was removing his wallet. After I bent down to pick them up, the three of you had vanished. I've been dashing around the station, searching for you like a giddy goat. Thank goodness I found you before it was too late."

Ruby's face softened, though her gaze remained hard. "Thank you so much, James," she said, glaring at Pixley. "And now we must be off. Sorry we cannot stay to chat but I have no doubt we'll meet up with you soon in Oxford."

Fina shuddered at the thought.

"Oh, you'll see me sooner than that," he said with a low chuckle. "I have the berth next to you two." He nodded to Ruby and Fina. "Jolly good. We'll have a ripping time on the train, won't we?"

"Marvellous," mumbled Pixley under his breath.

"What's that, old boy?" said James, slapping Pixley on his back. His voice was pitched nervously high and the slap connected just a little too heavily for comfort.

Pixley winced. "I said, that's marvellous you'll be joining us, James. What a splendid adventure."

Ruby trotted toward platform seven. As they dashed after her, Fina said, "How on earth can you afford to take *Train Blanc* as a student, James?"

"I've come into some money. A bit of a flutter at the roulette wheel in Monte, Feens," he said.

"I'd rather you didn't call me Feens," said Fina, holding on to her hat as they ran toward the line of people entering the train.

"Oh, right, sorry," he said, hanging his head like a scolded puppy. Suddenly, Fina was sorry for him. She had a sudden vision of him tearing scraps of paper and putting them discreetly in his mouth, as he had done in tense moments at Oxford. The boy must be considerably sensitive to strain. She put a hand on his shoulder. "Thanks so much for retrieving our tickets, James. I'm not sure what would have happened if you hadn't found us!"

Head still hanging low, James merely nodded. His face was hidden by the curtain of hair but there was something about the tilt of his jaw that suggested his eager grin had vanished. In fact, his posture looked positively downcast. Fina was just about to ask him what the matter was when he whirled around and rushed off without a word.

Well, they would see him again, no doubt – perhaps at closer quarters than they'd like. Scanning her ticket, Fina noted they were at the far end of the train, nearer the engine than the rear. Fortunately, it was a short distance, as the train only had a few passenger carriages. She knew it was costly and exclusive but she had never seen a train like this. Despite her nervous exhaustion, she admired the gleaming cars and the attendants' impeccable uniforms at each door. They joined the queue behind a threesome quarrelling about their compartments. The attendant, a young man about Fina's age, stood patiently next to the fussy group. The only sign of impatience was a clenched jaw. He must have become accustomed to the eccentricities and habits of the wealthy.

"Which compartments are we in, Mother?" whined a girl. She was a woman, to be sure, but was clearly going to act like a spoiled child.

A careworn though attractive woman in her fifties

said, "I'm afraid I cannot read them without my eyeglasses." She handed her tickets to the attendant.

"Where did you leave them this time, Mother?" asked the girl. "I swear you lose them on purpose – for vanity's sake."

The older woman ignored this comment. "Dot, why don't you sleep in my compartment and spend the day in Ridgewell's compartment? That way you can have the best of both worlds," she said in a soothing voice.

Next to the woman stood a young person, presumably Ridgewell. One eye peeked out from behind the tilted fedora. He took a long drag on a cigarette and then stamped it out on the platform, utterly oblivious to the chaotic scene unfolding in front of him.

"Because you snore, Mother. And don't call me 'Dot' around other people. You know I hate it."

'Dot' stood with her arms crossed, blocking the doorway. The young attendant touched her elbow, stifling his irritation. "Please, Mademoiselle, we must board the train. I must help these lovely people into their compartments as well," he said, pointing at Fina, Pixley, and Ruby. All three glowed at the word 'lovely'.

Dot turned to glare at them. Then she shrugged and boarded the train, but not before launching into a monologue about their sleeping accommodations.

"Appears it's going to be a long journey, doesn't it, Mademoiselle?" A voice tinged with a German accent came from behind Fina. She spied a man in a priest's uniform as she craned her neck. He was uncommonly attractive, with a broad grin, impish eyes and a mop of dark brown hair, streaked with a bit of grey. Of course, he would have to be a priest. But he was too old for her. He must be forty!

Fina pursed her lips and nodded affirmation. "Are you travelling to Paris?"

He glanced up and down the platform as if this gesture would give him the answer. "No, to Lausanne only I will travel. I live in Switzerland."

She was about to continue her line of questioning but was interrupted by the attendant. "I am your attendant, Mademoiselle, or Miss Aubrey-'aveloque," he said, slowly pronouncing each syllable of her name as he read it on his manifest. "My name is Julien Paquet, and I will be your attendant on our journey. Please do not hesitate to ask me for anything you require," he said with a little bow.

3

"Thank you, Monsieur Paquet," she replied – though he seemed too young to be a Monsieur. "This is my first time on this type of train – I mean – this expensive a train." She stopped, inhaled, and let out a stream of words. "What I mean is, I am delighted to come aboard and am sure I will require very little."

He gave her a grin which transformed his face into a diamond shape. "Of course, Mademoiselle," he said, helping her aboard as Ruby and Pixley followed behind.

Their merry crowd uttered spontaneous 'oohs' and 'ahhs' at the sumptuous compartment. The oak panelling was so polished Fina could rearrange her hair in it – a task that was never-ending for her. Even the chrome door handles sparkled. Fina was glad she wore gloves so she wouldn't spoil it with her fingerprints. Pixley was in the last cabin, number 12, and Ruby and

Fina shared number 11. Next door, number 10, was allotted to James.

"It's absolutely spiffing!" chirped Fina. The beds had been made into plush sofas covered in antimacassars. A wardrobe-like contraption in cherry wood stood across from it, next to an enclosed washstand in the corner. Near the window was a light with a pink beaded lampshade and a small box. It resembled something. Chocolate.

Fina dashed to the window ledge to inspect the box. She lifted the blue lid to find chocolates nestled underneath.

"Just like you to be the first one to find the chocolate," laughed Ruby. "And I'm glad you did. I need relief from the strain of our near debacle." She removed her hat and all but fell onto the sofa.

"Mmm..." said Fina with her mouth full. "Try these. Scrumptious. Must be Swiss." She handed the box over to Ruby, who rooted around to find her favourite piece. A caramel.

"Life is becoming better," said Ruby as she took a small bite of the chocolate. Fina didn't understand how she managed such small bites.

"Do you think Pixley really lost the tickets? Or did James swipe them?" asked Fina as she opened her suitcase.

Ruby tilted her head back into the sofa. "That was definitely my first thought when James turned up – like a bad penny."

"He is rather like a limpet, isn't he? At least he didn't nibble on the tickets before he gave them back to us," said Fina, shaking out one of her frocks before putting it on a hanger.

"How in heaven's name did he know we would be on this train?" asked Ruby, rooting around in the box for another caramel. They'd have to commandeer Pixley's chocolates – if he hadn't eaten them already, which Fina suspected he would have.

"Must be the same way he found out where we'd be in Sardinia." Fina shivered. "Makes me think there must be a network of spies. Which also makes me wonder why you were so keen to take this train. Do you know something that I don't?"

"Ian sent us these tickets when we were in Florence, saying we must take this train back to London. He gave me no further explanation in his letter, though I'm certain you believe I'm withholding something," Ruby said.

"Well, you do go all misty-eyed on me whenever his name is mentioned," giggled Fina.

Ian Clavering, theatre producer and sometime who-knows-what-kind-of-spy, was the one person who could melt Miss Ruby Dove's iron resolve. Besides her dear brother, Wendell, of course. Fina liked Ian but disapproved of his disappearing acts. But she wasn't one to judge since her would-be suitors all seemed to vanish.

Perhaps she would bump into Charles or Idris in London. *When pigs fly,* she thought, bitterly.

"But to answer your question," continued Ruby, ignoring Fina's comment about Ian, "he gave us these tickets and said we were not to switch compartments under any circumstances."

"Sounds ominous."

Pixley poked his head in through the door. "How are you doing, girls?"

He was probably the only person in the world who could call Fina a girl and not receive a glare.

Pixley wiped away a smear of chocolate from the corner of his mouth. So much for the extra chocolates. Fina sighed. When would dinner be served? Maybe they would have a nibble before then.

"I've never even seen a train like this from the outside," said Ruby, staring around again in awe. "And the inside is even better. What's yours like, Pixley?"

"The same as yours. And I notice we had the same box of chocolates," he said, rubbing his belly. "But I'll need a bit more before dinner. Did Julien tell you what time they serve dinner?"

"I expect the conductor will notify us," said Ruby.

And as if he had been summoned, a man in a conductor's cap appeared. Fina took an instant liking to this man, even though she disapproved of his enormous salt-and-pepper moustache. He tipped his cap then checked his clipboard and said, "Good afternoon, Miss

Dove, Miss Aubrey-Havelock and Mr Hayford. My name is Laurent Belrose, and I am the conductor on this journey to Paris. I will be at your service at almost any time of the day or the night, along with our attendant, who you have already met – Julien Paquet."

"This is a small train, but that seems like a small staff, even for twelve compartments," said Pixley.

Laurent's mouth set in a grim line as he shrugged. "Yes. The only other member of the staff – except for the engine driver and his assistant – is our chef, Maurice Gaudin. Are you familiar with the celebrated Chef Gaudin?" he asked, peering at each of them, one by one.

They all shook their heads.

"I'm afraid we're not used to travelling in this style, nor eating famous French cuisine," said Fina.

"Ah well, then you're in for a treat!" he exclaimed, drawing his fingers together and then using them to blow a kiss. His face flashed into a frown. "Yes, we are very – how do you say? – short-staffed on this voyage. One of our Italian colleagues was called away to his sick mother in Brindisi. We did not succeed in finding someone to take his place at the last moment."

"Well, we'll be careful not to be an additional burden to your load," said Ruby.

He gave a little sighing hiccough of relief at Ruby's statement. "I am glad to hear this, but please do ask me for anything you might need."

"Do you have a timetable of our arrival schedule? I

enjoy finding out where we are when we arrive at different stations," she said as if the request needed an explanation.

"But of course, of course, Mademoiselle," he said, dipping into the bag on his shoulder. "Here is a detailed timetable up until we arrive in Paris the day after tomorrow."

"Do you expect any snow along the way?" asked Pixley like an excited child.

Laurent peered at Pixley as if he were as high as two hats. "Snow. Yes. Most assuredly, though I am confident the tracks will remain clear, given the weather report. But you will enjoy plenty of snow, don't worry," he said, rubbing the back of his neck. "This is the last train of the season before the mountain route becomes impassable."

He scanned his clipboard, as if he was searching for something. He held up a finger. "Ah, yes, the dinner, I must tell you, it will be served at seven o'clock. In the meantime, if you desire tea or coffee, it is being served in the dining room until six o'clock." Then he paused and gave a little chuckle.

"I see by your faces that you three will be the first ones in the dining room."

4

As they made their way toward the dining car, Fina had to peek in the compartments they passed.

Soft snoring floated from James' cabin. He had looked haggard in the train station. Through the next door over, number 9, all Fina saw was a flurry of clothes flying about as the passenger unpacked. She could tell the person was petite and had long dark hair, but that was all.

The doors to numbers 8 and 7 were shut.

Fina steadied herself as the train carriage swayed over a rough patch of rail. They were leaving the station. Rain spattered the window and tapped softly on the roof. The effect was calming and pleasing.

Meow.

Ruby looked over her shoulder, as did Pixley, in a seriocomic gesture. "What was that? A baby? Oh good

Lord, I hope there isn't a baby on the train," he said, sighing.

Fina glared at Pixley. "I like babies," she said. "But I suppose they can be quite trying on a train."

"I thought it sounded like a cat," said Ruby.

They halted their progress. Fina leaned her head against the door. There it was again. *Meow.*

"It's definitely a cat," said Fina. "What fun! We must ask Julien or Laurent about it."

In the second sleeping carriage, cabin 6 housed a grandmotherly woman in a sensible wool suit. Her long hair was pulled back into an enormous bun. She hummed to herself gently while she knitted an indeterminate item of sickly-pink clothing.

The rest of the cabin doors were shut. With few mishaps – other than Pixley's round spectacles falling to the floor – they arrived at the lounge car.

Fina gasped. It was more splendid than she could have ever imagined. It had the ambience of a stately but lived-in drawing room, with paintings hung at each end of the carriage. Small mahogany tables were interspersed among the red-and-gold upholstered furniture which lined the walls. Several were already occupied. In one sat the laconic fellow they'd seen on the train platform, whose mother had called him Ridgewell. A sketchbook was balanced on his knee and, despite the jolting of the train, he was making quick, sure strokes on the paper with a small stick of charcoal.

Nearest to Fina sat a man of around sixty. Good lord, the man had a monocle! His military bearing and monocle made him appear much older than he probably was. His eyes furrowed as he peered down at his half-empty – or half-full – crossword. He had a healthy paunch and the florid appearance typical of pale-skinned people who are habitual drinkers.

His body jolted as he noticed Ruby, Pixley, and Fina. "God's teeth! You gave me a fright," he said. He popped up out of his seat like a man much younger, and much smaller in girth.

"Governor Wistow. Eustace Wistow," he said, sticking out his hand to Fina first.

"Pleased to meet you, ah, Governor, or shall I call you Mr Wistow?" said Fina.

"Wistow is fine, Miss, ah…" He peered more closely at her chest, as if that would provide the answer.

"Miss Aubrey-Havelock. But you may call me Fina. And these are my friends," she said, introducing Ruby and Pixley.

Mr Wistow shook their hands and gave an awkward bow. He clasped his hands together. "What do you all say to a game of bridge?"

"Sounds lovely, Mr Wistow, but perhaps later tonight. We're famished. We're on our way for tea. I see it's at the other end of the lounge," said Fina, hoping this would make for a smooth exit from Mr Wistow's company. He nodded and took a swig of his drink of choice from a cut-glass tumbler. "Good show, good show."

They moved off. "That man is decidedly from the Victorian era," murmured Pixley. "A classic fossilised relic."

Ruby gave him a playful nudge in the ribs.

But once again they were thwarted in their quest by a blockage in the aisle. Ridgewell had set aside his sketchbook and was leaning right over toward the next table, to carry on a lively conversation with ... the man in the navy suit who had bumped into Pixley. Fortunately, the two were so engaged that they both leaned back to make way without glancing at the passers-by.

Though Fina was always driven by her stomach, she was curious about this man in the navy suit. Something about him had jolted Ridgewell out of the laconic pose he had struck on the station platform; now, Ridgewell was scarcely the quiet one in this conversation. He threw up his hands and nodded excessively at his conversation partner. As for the man in the navy suit, he too was engrossed, but there was a practised quality about his body language. His chiselled face was not so animated as Ridgewell's baby face. His suit certainly fitted him well. It hung on his frame as if it were a second skin.

As they finally reached their goal, Pixley stopped. He leaned over to whisper in Fina's ear, "I've seen that man somewhere – the one in the navy suit."

Fina whispered in return, "Yes, he's the one who so rudely hit you when he passed by us on the platform."

"No, you goose," he smiled. "I know that. I mean somewhere else." He twirled his spectacles.

Ruby offered Fina a cup of tea. "Thank you. Are there any biscuits?" asked Fina. But Ruby was already handing her a plate piled high with those delicious-looking appetite-satisfiers.

The trio selected a wrap-around sofa in the corner, near the tea and coffee service. Through the rain-spattered window, Fina watched the outskirts of Genoa go by, dotted with red houses and black roofs. Her tour of Italy had been fantastic – minus the nightmare on Agrodoce island. She would be glad to return home to her cosy room at Oxford.

As she surveyed the governor drifting off to sleep on the opposite side of the lounge, Dot and her mother entered. Dot's mid-length hair was fashionably cut, as was her stylish burgundy-and-cream frock. But the whole effect was forced, somehow. You could tell she had put a great deal of effort into being fashionable, with the effect being one of grasping rather than ease. Her mother, on the other hand, seemed comfortable with herself – but she stooped over slightly, making her appear short.

Dot sat down across from her brother without an invitation. Her mother followed suit. Ridgewell shot a glance at his sister but continued to speak in low tones to the man in the navy suit.

"Aren't you going to introduce me to this charming man, Ridgewell?" Dot's voice had a slight adenoidal quality to it, as well as being high-pitched. Out of the corner of her eye, Fina saw Ruby cringe.

Ridgewell rose and gave an exaggerated bow toward his mother and sister. "May I introduce Etienne Durand. Mr Durand, this is my sister Dorothy and my mother, Mrs Synge."

"Please call me Madeline," said Mrs Synge.

Etienne bounced out of his seat and kissed each woman on the hand. Mother and daughter exchanged approving glances.

"That's it!" hissed Pixley to Ruby and Fina, "Etienne Durand. I've seen his photo in the paper several times. He's a high-ranking French diplomat. I recall he had a connection with the Soviets."

"Intriguing," said Ruby as she bit into another biscuit. "I wonder if he's coming to or from negotiations."

Their teacups slid perilously close to the edge of the table as the train snaked around a bend. But the woman who entered needed no assistance in balancing herself. Even from this end of the lounge car, the *Nuit de Longchamp* perfume wafted more quickly toward them than the wearer herself. And waft was indeed the correct word to describe her gait. Saunter and waft combined.

It was the woman from the platform, now minus her green beret, along with her companion in the burgundy suit.

Ruby leaned over the table and said, "Feens, she'd be an ideal one for our dress designs. We have the next day or so to convince her."

"What a vamp," said Pixley, surveying her not in disgust but awe.

The couple made their way toward them, nodding politely at the other passengers. Fina watched as all eyes followed the woman toward the coffee. She must have been in her early forties, and the young man in his early twenties. Well, well. Good for her.

Without warning, Mrs Synge jolted upright, and her hands flew to her cheeks. "Good Lord!" she gasped.

5

"Dot! Dot!" Mrs Synge continued in a stage whisper, pointing at the sultry woman in satin.

"What is it, Mother? What are you blubbering about?" said Dot, eyeing her mother up and down as if she were a shameful secret.

"It's – it's *Sophia Salazar*!" hissed Mrs Synge.

Sophia twirled around at the mention of her name. She smiled. No, she smirked.

"How charming that you recognised me," she said, gliding toward Mrs Synge.

Everyone else had blank looks on their faces.

"Surely you must all be familiar with Sophia Salazar," said Mrs Synge, appealing to the crowd with her hands. "The famous author..."

And then Mrs Synge fell silent. She shrank back into her shell. How peculiar.

Sophia's smile transformed from insincere to genuine. "Please do not distress yourself," she said to Mrs Synge. Then she turned to the crowd in the lounge. "This lovely lady has remembered why she knows me so well."

Everyone blinked.

Sophia's companion spoke for the first time. "Sophia Salazar is a famous Portuguese author of erotic fiction," he said in a strong French accent.

Gasps.

Ruby and Pixley giggled.

Mrs Synge's face was now a dull shade of brick-red. Dot turned to Madeline. "Mother!"

Mrs Synge's response was to fold her hands in her lap and look adequately scandalised.

Ridgewell said, "Good for you, Mother."

Sophia's companion, taking pity on Mrs Synge's embarrassment, intervened. "And I am Miss Salazar's secretary, Raoul Lapointe."

Dot stared at him, as did Ridgewell. He was indeed handsome. His eyelids had a way of remaining at half-mast, giving the face an appearance of casual insouciance. But he was a little too handsome for Fina's tastes. Ruby and Pixley felt the same way, judging by their faces.

The man in the navy suit cleared his throat, rose, and gave Miss Salazar a little bow. "It is a great pleasure to meet you, Miss Salazar and Mr Lapointe. I am Etienne Durand."

"The pleasure is all mine," simpered Sophia as she gazed at Etienne. Etienne gulped and ran a finger around his collar. If he were disappointed that she didn't recognise his name, he didn't show it.

Ruby whispered, "She's marvellous. She can make even a diplomat nervous."

The table quivered. It couldn't be the train, since they were on a long, calm stretch of track. Fina peered down at Pixley's jiggling leg.

"What are you writing, Pixley?" she asked as he scribbled in a small notepad.

"Hmmm?" he said, looking up and pushing back his spectacles. "Oh, I'm writing notes. Perhaps I can cajole Etienne into giving me a story."

"You're shameless, Pixley Hayford," said Ruby.

"Shameless yourself, dear one," he smiled. "Aren't you about to try to hook a new client?"

Indeed, Ruby fawned over Sophia's travelling suit as they did their best to gracefully exit the lounge.

But not before Fina had spilt tea all over her own frock.

"I'm afraid I'll need your famous – or infamous – stain-remover, Ruby. Have you any with you?"

"Of course. Even though it makes me shudder every time I think of it."

Pixley's head turned around from the front of their line. "How can stain-remover be infamous?"

"I'll tell you later about our adventures at Pauncefort Hall. Now, let's return to our compartment sometime before the autumn term at Oxford is over," said Ruby.

"Impatience is not a virtue in a young lady," said Pixley in his best imitation of a schoolteacher's voice. He giggled at his own impression.

"Oxford?" came a voice from behind them.

The voice belonged to someone they hadn't yet met. It was the dark-haired woman who had been trapped in a typhoon of clothes in her compartment. She had wide eyes, long dangling earrings, and a beautiful top which clashed with her gorgeous skirt. Here was a woman who enjoyed clothes, but needed assistance in how to arrange them.

She held out her hand to Ruby. "My name is Neeya Arafa. I heard you mention Oxford. Are you from Oxford?"

"This is Fina, and I'm Ruby – we both study at Oxford. I study chemistry and Fina studies political history."

"And I'm just a general dogsbody," said Pixley with a grin.

"Oh, so sorry, Pixley," said Ruby. "This is Mr Pixley Hayford, journalist extraordinaire!"

Pixley seemed mollified by this pronouncement, but

somewhat disappointed by the lack of reaction from Neeya.

"I'm sure you're quite famous, Mr Hayford—"

"Pixley is fine," he replied.

"Pixley, then. I was about to say I'm sure you're famous, but I've been in Cairo for many years, so I'm unlikely to have read any of your stories."

"Why were you interested in Oxford?" asked Fina.

"For two reasons. One, I was at a boarding school near Oxford when I was a girl. Second, while I'm not on my way to Oxford, I am on my way to begin my PhD studies at a university in Brussels."

"How impressive," said Ruby. "Did you finish your degree in Cairo?"

Her eyes slid downward. "Yes, as an undergraduate, as well as my law degree."

"Wait a moment!" cried Pixley. "I've heard of you. Weren't you the first woman to finish her law degree in Egypt?"

A broad smile flashed across Neeya's face but vanished as she did her best to appear modest. "Yes, that's me."

"Are you leaving because of the unrest over the past year?" asked Fina.

Ruby grimaced.

Neeya brushed a wisp of hair from her face. "It has made it easier to contemplate leaving home, but it was not the reason. I wanted to see a bit of the world, and I thought Brussels would be a good first step."

She stepped aside as Dot tapped her on the shoulder.

"Mother!" squawked Dot from behind them. "Come along!"

Like a gaggle of geese, the Synge clan descended on them, pushing forward through the corridor.

Ruby held up her hand as if she were drowning in water. "Pleased to meet you, Miss Arafa!"

Fina mumbled to Pixley, "These Synges are vying for most irritating guests already."

The last thing Fina saw was Pixley's bald head, bobbing in affirmation, before the lights flickered, hissed, and died.

6

———

A screech of brakes, a loud thud, and then silence.

The train shuddered to a grinding halt. The darkness was complete, with not even a far-off lamp visible through the windows.

Someone screamed. Was it Dot?

Shuffling ensued. A sharp pain shot up Fina's back.

"Ow!"

"Sorry," came the voice. Ridgewell. "I'm so sorry. I fell on you."

"No one panic," said Pixley in a rich baritone. "Everyone stay where you are. I'm sure the conductor will come to find us in a moment."

Sure enough, the steady voice of Laurent came through to them from the front of the coach. Torchlight shone on them. Fina squinted at the faces around her. Everyone appeared genuinely surprised.

"Ladies and gentlemen, please do not worry yourselves. Three events came together to make this happen. A signal told us to come to an abrupt halt, which, unhappily, was inside a tunnel. We had a temporary power cut as a result."

"What kind of train is this? I thought this was the famous *Train Blanc*," said Dot.

"I offer my apologies for the inconvenience, Miss Synge. Fortunately, I have a few torches on hand to give to you," he said. Soon Ruby had a torch in hand, as did three other passengers.

"I suggest you find your way back to your cabins and stay there until we restore power. That should occur shortly," he said, his vocal cords straining to a high pitch.

Mumbling ensued, but everyone followed the conductor's orders.

When they reached Pixley's compartment he said, "Let's go into my cabin. I have matches and candles."

"You are a man of surprises," said Ruby. "Let's see if we can contact the spirits," she giggled.

Pixley wasn't exaggerating when he said he had candles, plural. Soon the compartment resembled a soothsayer's séance room or some other place of holy rituals.

"This is cosy," said Ruby.

"That's one of the many things I love about you,

Ruby," said Fina. "You find the bright side to a misfortune."

"Well, I've had plenty of practice at that, Feens," she replied. Then, her voice brightening, she said, "But thank you for the compliment."

"I say," said Pixley. "This calls for a drink!" He rummaged around in his suitcase and soon held a flask aloft.

"Were you in the Girl Guides as a child, Pixley?" asked Ruby.

His spectacles lifted on his nose as he smiled. "No, but let's say that as a journalist worth his salt, you must be prepared for anything. I travel light, but I'm always prepared."

As good as his word, he removed a small nested metal cylinder, which popped up into a funnel-like cup. They took turns sipping the brandy.

"What do you think of the crowd so far?" asked Ruby.

"I'm not sure what I expected, but it does seem to be an eclectic group," said Pixley. "That Dot woman will be trying, I can tell. I'd almost rather have a screaming infant than her."

"Too right," laughed Fina. "What is their story? The family, I mean."

"Probably aristocratic wastrels and layabouts with nothing better to do than trundle between London and the Riviera," he spat.

"My, my, someone is grumpy," said Ruby. "Here, have another sip of brandy." He obliged. Then her head snapped up, alert. "Wait," she whispered. "Do you hear something?"

Something was scratching at their door.

Pixley sprang toward the door.

"Meeoow…"

A white kitten – with a large caramel splotch sitting on it like a saddle – lifted one paw as if to scratch on the door again.

Collective cooing issued forth from the trio.

Fina pounced on the kitten before Ruby and Pixley reached the little ball of fur. She cradled it in her arms like a baby.

"You ought to be a mother, Feens. You're a natural," said Ruby.

"Very funny," replied Fina, scratching the kitten's head. "What's your name, little one?" she said to the cat, peering down at its collar.

Fina could scarcely run her finger between the cat's neck and the gold braided collar. The kitten purred as she rubbed its neck. At the end of the collar hung a silver heart pendant.

"An adorable pendant, but it's a bit too heavy for this poor kitten's head," said Fina.

"It will build her neck muscles," said Pixley.

"Don't be beastly, Pixley," said Ruby, as Fina did her best to adjust the collar so it wasn't strangling the kitten.

The kitten struggled and bounced to the floor. It jumped onto Pixley's legs and kneaded its claws into his wool trousers.

"Hey there! You!" he said, tossing the kitten at Ruby. The kitten's paw caught one of the candles mid-air, sending both tumbling over. A small conflagration erupted on the carpet. In his haste to move away from the fire, Pixley dumped the cup of brandy onto the floor, directly onto the flames.

"Bloody hell!" yelled Pixley as the fire leapt up, hissing and sparking.

Ruby dashed into the hallway, torch in hand, and soon returned with a fire extinguisher. She sprayed the flames, dousing the kitten, Fina and Pixley. The cat screeched, with Fina and Pixley not far behind.

Thudding footsteps approached.

"*Mon Dieu!*" yelled Laurent.

Raoul's head popped out of his cabin, right behind the conductor. "There you are, little one. How did you escape the compartment, Ricki?" he said in a scolding voice.

"Is this your cat?" demanded Pixley, wiping away the extinguisher spray from his spectacles in a fury.

"Yes, so sorry if he disturbed you. He's a kitten so he tries to escape whenever he can."

Ricki gave a pitiful mew as he licked his fur dry. As Fina realised she would need to change anyway, she focused on the cat. After retrieving a wet towel from the washstand, she cleaned the kitten. Who knew what kind of poisons were in the fire extinguisher? Then she dried him so well she could barely spot his nose through the puffy fur.

"He's welcome any time," said Fina, handing the kitten to Raoul with reluctance. Ricki crawled onto Raoul's chest.

Ruby and Pixley glared at Fina. She shrugged. "Or I ought to say, I'd be glad to cat-sit in your cabin should you need me."

Raoul gave her the secret smile of one cat-lover to another. Then his smile vanished. "Thank you for your offer, Miss Aubrey-Havelock, but Ricki should stay with me at all times." He paused and said, "You understand, it is for his own good. As you can see, he's already caused a minor emergency."

Laurent threw up his hands at the scene. "It's official. This train is cursed," he said. Then he knocked on the oak panelling.

As if in response to his statement, the lights flickered on and the low rumble of the engine echoed around the cabin.

7

With the lights gaining in brightness, everyone cheered. At least this experience had brought them all a little closer together. Not that one needed to be so close during a two-day train journey.

"Dinner is served!" announced Laurent, his moustache curving into a smile. "Maurice told me that as soon as they had restored power we could seat everyone in the dining car."

After Ruby and Pixley had changed out of their wet clothes, they trundled along to the dining car. By the look of things, they were the last ones to arrive. A sense of frivolity – probably from relief, Fina surmised – pervaded the coach. The bubbly flowed, along with conversation, which had already risen to a fever-pitch.

The only quiet one was the grandmotherly woman Fina had observed knitting earlier. She peered out of the window, watching the scenery quite contentedly. The view consisted only of pinpricks of light occasionally interrupted by a burst of light from a passing village. The grandmother looked like she was not even aware of the commotion around her.

Julien piloted the trio to sit with the grandma, as the other seats were occupied.

"Hello, *Schätze*," she said to each of them after they had introduced themselves. "My name is Ada Hartman. Ada will do."

Fina was a little shocked by the casual use of the term of endearment in German. But then again, one was free to do whatever one pleased at that age, wasn't one?

"Are you from Germany or Switzerland? Or perhaps Austria?" asked Fina.

Their glasses of champagne arrived. Fina pounced on hers, but not before Pixley had drained his in one gulp. "Steady on, Pixley," whispered Ruby. His only response was to smile and signal to Julien for a top-up.

"I'm from Braunschweig – in Germany."

"Doesn't ring a bell, but I've always wanted to travel to Germany," said Fina wistfully. "Isn't Berlin a non-stop party? I'm not particularly fond of large parties, but I love the atmosphere."

Ada shook her head. "It is a delightful city, but I'm afraid it's being ruined by those thugs. And that ghastly set of laws they passed," she said, her little hands balling into fists.

"You mean the so-called Nuremberg laws?" Ruby shuddered. "I've heard of them."

"Yes, those bastards—"

Pixley, Ruby and Fina all stared at this sweet little grandmother.

"Oh dear, *Mäuschen*, I see I've upset you with my language," she laughed. "Young people are so sensitive these days." Then she banged her fist on the table. "But those bastards have the nerve to pass these dangerous laws. It will not end well, mark my words," she pronounced.

"No, it certainly won't. Not after what the Germans did to the Herero and Namaqua in German-controlled southwest Africa," said Pixley, shaking his head. "I've been working on a long-term story about the camps the Germans used to kill thousands of native peoples in retaliation for their resistance. The British government published a report about it in 1918, but ordered all copies destroyed ten years later."

"I wonder if it had anything to do with shameful British atrocities in India, dear friend?" said Ruby.

"Well," said Fina, "it feels odd to say this when I'm the one who's interested in politics, but how about we move on to a brighter subject? Especially since we all appear to agree."

And, as if on cue, Julien appeared with the soup.

The table behind Fina had already finished their soup and were chatting away.

"Governor, you say? Governor of what?" asked the priest.

"Former governor, thank goodness," said Eustace. "I was governor of the Leeward Islands – Antigua, Montserrat, Nevis, St Kitts, and Saint Christopher, among others."

Ruby's soup spoon clattered into her bowl, splashing soup all over her and Ada.

"Oh, I'm so dreadfully sorry, Mrs Hartman," said Ruby, wetting a napkin and offering it to Ada.

Ada peered at Ruby. "No trouble, my dear. But something has upset you. I can tell you're not the kind of young woman who drops her spoon in her soup," she said as she wiped her frock. "Tell Oma Ada all about it."

And just like that, Ruby spilt forth everything about St Kitts, her home. The ongoing tragedies of the plantation system, the role of the British government and commercial interests, and the violent repression of worker revolts. All of it. Including a story about how police killed her cousin during the so-called Buckley's Strike earlier that year. Plantation owners had refused to raise cane-workers' wages, so the workers went on strike. The series of events that led to escalating violence between the workers and plantation management was in dispute but at some point, the government intervened. Three people had died, including Ruby's cousin, Olive.

Fina sat, stunned. She had never seen Ruby reveal so

much of what was important to her to a total stranger. But that was the power of this little old lady, Oma Ada.

Pixley must have felt the same way because he turned, ever so slowly, and stared at Fina, nodding toward Ruby and Ada. Then he promptly downed the next glass of bubbly.

"Julien, would you bring me a scotch?"

Fina tried not to glance at Pixley. Though she had not been friends with him very long, she knew he was usually a social drinker, not a heavy drinker. Something must be on his mind.

A delicious smell wafted to the table. The main course arrived. Julien said, "Chicken Basquaise – a special request of Miss Salazar." Fina's eyes rolled back in her head when she took the first bite.

They had all soon gobbled up everything in sight. Pixley lit a cigarette, but not before offering one to Fina. What was going on? Pixley didn't smoke.

Well, no point in being a cowardly custard. "Pixley, I have to ask. Are you under a particular strain right now? I've never seen you smoke," she said, thinking it wise not to mention the alcohol.

He coughed on the cigarette. Fina couldn't help but laugh a bit.

"Are you laughing at me, Miss Aubrey-Havelock?"

"No, no, never, Mr Hayford." Fina smiled.

His face turned grave. "I do have something on my mind. I'm keen to share, like our dear friend across the table," he said, waving smoke in Ruby's direction. Ruby was so engrossed in conversation with Ada that she noticed neither the reference to herself nor the smoke wafting into her face. "But I'm afraid I have to keep mum about it for the moment. Please don't be hurt by it – it has nothing to do with trusting you," he said, placing his hand over his heart.

"*Le dessert*?" asked Julien, materialising out of nowhere. He smirked, knowing full well what the answer would be.

"Yes," the four of them answered in unison.

"I propose to you mille-feuilles, stewed peaches, crepes in Calvados, or assorted cheese."

Fina and Ada selected mille-feuilles, while Pixley and Ruby opted for the crepes.

A finger tapped Fina's shoulder.

"I say, do you all fancy a game of bridge in the lounge once we've finished?" asked the governor, tilting his chair back a little too far. Pixley didn't turn his head but Father Felix Schweinsteiger, at another table, half-turned in his chair at the words.

"Oh, ah, perhaps, Mr Wistow," said Fina. "I'm afraid I'm hopeless at bridge. And I don't believe my partners..."

"I'll play bridge, *Herr* Governor," piped up Ada from the corner.

The governor sighed. "Ah, splendid, Mrs Hartman.

Good show and all that..." He trailed off, clearly disappointed.

Fina gave a grateful smile to Ada. She winked back at her.

Ruby leaned over the table to form a huddle. "Thank you for rescuing Fina – and the rest of us – Mrs Hartman. But most especially Fina. I have a feeling she might have socked the dear governor one for good measure. Our dear little Miss Aubrey-Havelock has violent tendencies."

Pixley laughed so hard his chin shook. He removed his spectacles and wiped his eyes clear of tears of laughter. Then he laid a calming hand on Fina's arm. "I'm so sorry, Fina. I just remembered when you gave Mr Gasthorpe a right hook in Oxford. I'm in total admiration of you."

Ada gave Fina a nod of approval. "I have a sixth sense about people. I knew you were special, Miss Aubrey-Havelock. Like Miss Dove here," she said, patting Ruby's hand. "And I'm sure Mr Hayford as well."

After she had savoured the smooth, velvety goodness of her mille-feuille, Ada rose abruptly from her seat and knocked on the table. "It's time for bridge. And other card games, if I've had enough to drink."

8

The guests toddled after Ada into the lounge. Julien had already set out decks of cards. There were even poker chips stacked in the corner. Ada, Dot, Governor Eustace and Father Felix arranged themselves around the largest table and began a lively round of bridge.

Ruby, Fina and Pixley, meanwhile, ensconced themselves in the middle of the lounge, mostly out of an eavesdropping habit. They could still hear everyone above Noël Coward's *Mrs Worthington*, warbling from the gramophone.

Ruby and Fina opted for hot cocoa, while Pixley stayed faithful to his scotch. Fina had hoped that discussing whatever was worrying him might relieve the strain – but the opposite seemed to have occurred. Smoking like a chimney, he filled one small ashtray on the table in no time. He then leaned over and asked

Raoul for a cigarette. At least he appeared to be enjoying himself.

The train was already a hotbed of intrigue, from Fina's perspective. Ridgewell and Raoul sat in one corner, laughing, chatting, and drinking. Together, they flicked through the pages of Ridgewell's sketchbook, with Raoul giving little murmurs of appreciation. "Never again will I say the English have not the soul artistic," he exclaimed in his French lilt. "Your mother – you have put her on the page, alive!" He held up the sketchpad so that the bridge-players could see it, letting the pages riffle open. The faces of various train passengers flashed by, drawn in charcoal. Ridgewell certainly did have talent. Fina couldn't help craning her neck for a glimpse of herself.

Sophia Salazar and Madeline Synge also fawned over one another. What a curious couple. Madeline, resplendent in a beautifully-cut azure silk caftan, sat up straight for the first time, gesticulating wildly and throwing back one brandy after another. Sophia's posture, on the other hand, looked relaxed. Even though she wore a slinky evening gown, it looked as though she was putting her *femme fatale* persona on the shelf for a few minutes. They nattered away about Sophia's books.

Fina leaned over to Sophia when there was a natural lull in the conversation. "Miss Salazar, do you have any copies of your books with you? I'd love to peruse one of them – I didn't pack any reading material."

Sophia sucked on her cigarette and then blew a smoke ring toward the ceiling. Fina swore it resembled a heart. "But of course, Fina. I always carry at least one slim volume with me for just such eventualities." She slid a novella from her handbag without hesitation.

The cover splashed the words *Scarlet Sash* in violent red. Sophia's mouth curved up at one corner. "This is my private version. I find that publishing them in English has been the most lucrative. And the version sold to the public has to have, well, a less explicit cover, you understand."

Fina gulped and flipped through the book, though the pages flew so rapidly that the words were just a blur.

"Your scarlet face shows you will enjoy this little volume," said Sophia with a burbling laugh.

Pixley, who had been engrossed in watching the bridge game – or at least staring at it in a stupor – turned toward Fina. "I forgot to buy a few books before boarding the train. May I borrow yours?"

Ruby laughed. Then Fina burst out laughing. Pixley seemed puzzled.

"May we join you?" asked Etienne. Neeya popped up behind him.

"We'd be delighted," said Ruby.

"I say!" exclaimed Pixley, as if this were the first time he'd laid eyes on Etienne. "You were the chappie who so rudely ploughed into me at the train station!"

Etienne furrowed his brow and sipped on his glass

of port. Then he put a palm to his forehead. "Ah! But I am so sorry – I'm desolated. Please accept my most heart-full – I mean heartfelt – apologies. I was preoccupied with a matter of importance and also late for this train. When those two things happen at the same time, I'm afraid I become oblivious to everything around me. Which is odd as I am a naturally observant person."

"Apologies accepted, old man, apologies accepted," said Pixley. He clinked his glass with Etienne's port glass, nearly causing it to topple over. "What are you doing on this train, anyway?"

Pixley's eyes darted from side to a side in a rapid motion. A sure sign he was beyond help.

Fina and Ruby shot one another a look. The look which said, 'We ought to do something.'

But Etienne responded to Pixley's question without hesitation. "I'm a diplomat for the French government. I had affairs of business to attend to in Genoa, but it was necessary that I return to Paris for negotiations."

"What kind of negotiations – may we ask?" queried Neeya.

Clearly, Etienne was a bit sozzled as well. "Well, I should not say, but they're high-level talks. With a major power."

"With whom, man, with whom?" demanded Pixley.

Ruby and Fina giggled.

"Well, with the Soviets, if you must know," said Etienne. Then, as if to soothe himself, he lit another cigarette. "It will undoubtedly be in the papers soon enough."

"Speaking of papers, would you consider an exclusive interview?" asked Pixley.

Etienne's cigarette slipped through his fingers to the floor. Pixley bent over and retrieved it before it caused any damage to the green carpet.

"You – you – you are a journalist?" asked Etienne as his eyebrows lifted toward the ceiling.

"You are shameless, Mr Hayford," said Ruby. But she smiled.

"I'm afraid so, Mr Durand," said Pixley. "I'm a journalist, not shameless. Well, perhaps just a bit shameless."

Etienne frowned.

"I can assure you, I am very professional, Mr Durand," said Pixley. He leaned toward Etienne. "I will be meticulous in reporting exactly what you say."

Etienne stared at Pixley, holding his gaze for at least ten seconds. Then he said, "Let me sleep on it, 'old man', let me sleep on it." He emphasised the words 'old man' carefully, as if they were explosive. He pursed his lips as if to signal the conversation officially over.

Fina glanced around the room to see that Raoul had pulled out a packet of tarot cards. Ridgewell spied Ruby and Fina looking in their direction and waved them over.

"Come join us," said Raoul. "I'm about to tell

Ridgewell's fortune." He placed the deck of cards on the table with long, spider-like fingers.

"Jolly good!" said Ridgewell, rubbing his hands together.

Raoul turned over each card with the seriousness of a croupier at a high-stakes card game in Monte.

"Hmmm..." said Raoul, rubbing his chin. "I see you were on a journey. Now you're beginning the first part of a new journey."

"Didn't need the occult to tell me that," said Ridgewell in a good-natured tone.

Raoul ignored his comment. "You are trying to balance two competing forces. It's not clear which one will win out," he pronounced.

The smirk disappeared from Ridgewell's face.

"And you have some sort of longing in your life – an important relationship?"

Ridgewell sat transfixed, staring at the cards.

Raoul had finished. In the awkward silence that ensued, Ruby said, "May I be next, Mr Lapointe?"

Raoul grinned. "But of course, Miss Dove," he said, still staring at Ridgewell.

He performed the same operation with the reverence of a holy ritual. "You have had a great deal of turmoil in your life, Miss Dove. You are driven and ambitious. I see you are also on a journey but, unlike Mr Synge, you are well along your path. Many obstacles stand in your way."

"Is there anything in there about a relationship?" asked Fina, giggling.

Ruby glanced at Fina with a disapproving look. It only prompted Fina to laugh more.

Raoul smiled. "I see that relationships with family are amicable. In the romantic category, though, it looks as though you have had some challenges," he said.

"I'll say," said Fina.

"You're one to talk, Feens," said Ruby, nudging her playfully in the ribs. It was a little too close to home for both.

Etienne and Neeya wandered over to join them again. "May I be next?" asked Etienne.

Good lord, the man was blotto. This behaviour did not fit Fina's image of a high-level French diplomat.

Voices rose from the bridge table. "You cheated, you cheated!" yelled Dot like a petulant child.

The priest held his hands up in mock surrender. "Calm yourself, I did no such thing."

Eustace put a calming hand on Dot's shoulder. "No need to upset yourself, my dear. I'm sure it's a misunderstanding."

Dot glared at him and crossed her arms.

"Ahem." Ada cleared her throat. "Mr Eustace is correct. I'm sure it was a mistake."

"Well, misunderstanding or no misunderstanding, I'm off to bed," said Dot in a huff. "Have you got one of those magical sleeping tablets of yours, Wellers? I'll

need one if the train keeps jigging and jogging like this."
She rose and signalled to her mother and brother. They
followed. Sophia rose in her turn and wagged a finger at
Raoul. So much for having her own tarot reading,
thought Fina.

The disruption to the party was enough to prompt
other guests to consider turning in for the night as well.

As Ruby drained the rest of her cocoa, her eyes
widened. "I cannot believe we haven't noticed this until
now, but have you noticed who's been missing
all night?"

9

"James!" cried Pixley.

Fina motioned to Julien. He was lounging in the corner, enjoying a cigarette.

"Yes, Mademoiselle Aubrey-'avelock?"

"Have you seen Mr Matua all evening?"

Julien scratched his head. "No, but the young man was sleeping when I knocked on his cabin door to announce the dinner. He was snoring."

Pixley tapped his water glass with a pen. "Ahem. Ladies and gentlemen. Have any of you seen a young man with dark, floppy hair since you boarded the train?"

Shaking heads followed blank stares.

"I saw him board the train," said Sophia. "The last I saw of him was when he slipped into his own compartment."

Raoul said, "Ah, I did see him after that. I let Ricki play in the corridor for a few minutes. He was on his way to *les cabinets* but stopped to pet the kitten. How could anyone resist Ricki?"

"Anyone else?" asked Ruby.

Silence.

Ruby said, "Right. Would you accompany us, Mr Paquet? I'm concerned."

With a knot in her stomach, Fina followed the others to James's door. Julien tapped.

No answer.

"Mr Matua... Mr Matua?"

"You'd better open the door, Julien," said Pixley, suddenly sober. He added, "Don't worry – we are acquaintances, so we will take responsibility."

Julien turned the key in the lock. James lay on the sofa, eyes closed.

Julien approached and shook him gently. "Mr Matua, are you feeling ill?"

His eyes remained closed

Pixley moved to the sofa and sat James upright. He applied pressure to his wrist. "He's alive."

Ruby and Fina let out a great whoosh of air.

As Pixley gave his cheeks a soft slap, James's eyes fluttered. They opened at half-mast. "What? Why are you waking me? Where am I?"

Ruby disappeared and reappeared with a small bottle she handed to Pixley. "Smelling salts."

Waving the bottle underneath James's nose did the trick. His eyes opened fully now, though his head swayed, causing his hair to completely cover his eyes.

"What happened, James?" asked Fina.

"I – I – I boarded the train, laid out my clothes and then ate those chocolates," he said, pointing to the same box they had in their own compartments. "Then I fell asleep. What time is it?"

"Ten o'clock, sir," said Julien.

James goggled. "You mean I've been asleep for over six hours?" He buried his face in his hands. "Oh, crikey."

Pixley patted James's back. "You might have been drugged, old man. Did you take any pills or eat anything else?"

James rubbed his eyes. "No, no. Just the chocolates."

Ruby peered in the chocolate box and then showed it to Fina. It was empty. Little crumbs of chocolate rolled around in the bottom.

"Perhaps you accidentally had something before you boarded the train."

James shook his head but said, "I suppose so, but it's doubtful. I hadn't eaten lunch, which is why I ate the whole box of chocolates." His eyes flashed and he threw up his hands. "Are you doubting what I say?" His voice rose to a level Fina had never heard before. "Just go away. Leave me alone."

10

———

Ruby fluffed up her pillow.

"I can't sleep, Feens, and I hear by your tossing and turning that you can't, either."

Fina lifted her head and peered over the edge of the bed. The blood in her head rushed downward, making her woozy. "Do you want to switch bunks? I don't mind sleeping on either of them."

"No – thanks for letting me take the bottom one. My fear of heights can strike at any time."

"Is there a particular reason you have a fear of heights? Something that happened in your childhood?"

"I had many wonderful teachers in school, but I also had one who was particularly sadistic. If you were in trouble – or she thought you had done something wrong – she would march you into a tiny room on the top floor. It wasn't really that high, but to a child, everything seems dramatic. The room was so small – barely large enough for one child. For some odd reason, it had a window, so one had the sensation of being perched on a ledge."

"She sounds dreadful with a capital D."

"She was such a tyrant! Mrs Budge."

"Maybe she was eternally upset that her name was Budge," giggled Fina. "Sorry. I didn't mean to make light of it. May I ask what she thought you did that was wrong?"

"There was this irritating boy in my class. Algie was his name. Algie was as lazy and devious as they come. He would sit next to me and copy my work. I tried every-thing to keep him from doing it, but he always found a way to peek. I finally gave up caring or trying to hide my work from him. One day, Mrs Budge noticed – I have no idea why it took her so long – and she punished me for allowing Algie to cheat."

"What happened to Algie?"

"She sent him to the headmaster, but Algie didn't care because he spent most of his days in and out of that office."

"You must have been mortified."

"I was furious. And then felt guilty. And then was terrified when she put me in that room – for four hours!"

"I hope the school fired her before she could inflict her evilness on any other children," said Fina.

"Unfortunately, she became known as a fantastic disciplinarian. They made her headmistress of the school. But I had left by that point, thank goodness."

The train ran smoothly along the track. *Ca-clunk, ca-lunk.* Occasional flashes of light from passing stations peeped through the curtains.

"We must be going faster to make up for lost time."

"Mmhhh," said Ruby.

"What happened to James?"

"I suspect that's what's been keeping me awake. He became so defensive when we asked him questions about the chocolates. You don't suppose it's all a ruse?"

"You mean he faked being asleep and drugged?"

"Yes, though I don't know what that would achieve. Maybe he's avoiding someone?"

"But surely he cannot be absent for the entire journey ... could he?" asked Fina.

"But the alternative is even more rum – why would someone drug James?"

"Hmmm ... and another thing is bothering me," said Fina. "Pixley is worried about something. He told me he was when I asked him why he had taken up smoking."

"Is he worried about his job?"

"Mmmmhh..."

Ruby's tone indicated she was absent from the conversation. Could she be omitting something deliberately?

"Ruby?"

A light snore confirmed it was time for Fina to count sheep.

After a few more tosses and turns, she melted into unconsciousness.

Some hours later, Fina awoke with a jolt. She leaned over to the window and pulled back the curtains. A bright light glared in her face. As her eyes adjusted to the contrast, she saw dots of snow tumbling to the ground. A tiny, half-timbered station house door stood open as a few passengers passed through it.

The voices outside created a low, comforting rumble. She closed the curtains and lay back on her pillow.

Her eyes jerked open again. Water running. Was it coming from Pixley's compartment? What was he doing at this time of night? The water stopped and a few moments later she heard his cabin door open and close. She glanced at her watch. Five o'clock. Good grief. She turned over and drifted back to sleep, dreaming of chocolates and kittens.

11

———————

"Feens, time to rise and shine!"

Through her half-open eyes, Fina noticed Ruby had already dressed for the day.

"I will rise, but I will not shine," she mumbled, rubbing her eyes as she sat upright and bumped her head on the ceiling. Rubbing her head, she said, "See what happens when you rise and shine?"

"Sorry. It was good of you to let me have the lower bunk."

"What dreadful time of the morning is it?"

"Seven o'clock."

"But that's a travesty! Why get up so early when we have nothing to do?"

"I agree, but Laurent informed me that breakfast is served promptly at seven. They want to serve breakfast before they arrive at a particular station."

"It's criminal."

"Well, people could say we're criminal, too. Get a move on, lazybones."

Fina groaned and crawled down the ladder at a snail's pace. When she was on the second-to-last rung, the train lurched.

Then it pitched again and ground to a screeching halt.

Fina tumbled on to the floor on top of Ruby.

The blasted lights went out again.

"What the devil?" exclaimed Ruby.

"Selkies and kelpies. Bloody train."

"Are you injured, Feens?"

"No, I'll just have a few lovely bruises tomorrow."

A knock came from the wall.

"Must be Pixley," said Fina.

Ruby yelled, "Are you hurt, Pixley?"

He yelled back, "No, and you?"

"We're fine. We're coming to your compartment."

Light filtered through low-hanging clouds. At least they could find their bearings, unlike last night. But the corridor was preternaturally silent. Was everyone still asleep? Surely not. She heard Ricki mewing. Sophia and Raoul popped their heads out of their cabins. Raoul held Ricki in his arms.

"Has the train crashed?" asked Raoul.

Fina peered out of the window. Snow-tipped peaks, partially covered by clouds, indicated they had arrived in the Alps. A few snowflakes brushed against the window and then descended into a valley. They were on a bridge. She unfastened a window and poked her head out. Looking downward, she jerked her head back. It seemed to be miles to the ground. The specks in the valley might be houses, but she couldn't be sure.

"Better you than me, Feens," whispered Ruby. "Thank you – what do you see?"

"Well, the good news is I can't detect any derailed cars or obvious damage. The bad news is we're on a bridge, and the rear half of the train is in a tunnel," she said, turning back toward Ruby's ashen face. She put an arm on hers. "I'm sure it's temporary. Maybe they jumbled the train signals. I don't think we're in any danger."

When Ruby turned away, reassured, Fina gulped. The train was perched at a precarious height. Best not to tell Ruby too much about that.

A small crowd had gathered around them. Sophia wore a scarlet silk dressing gown, Raoul a green suit, and Neeya a casual frock. Pixley was dressed in a wool suit, bulwarked against the cold. But then he wiped his head with a handkerchief. Must be nerves.

Laurent dashed down the corridor toward them. "Please, ladies and gentlemen. Do not alarm yourselves. I will explain all once we're assembled in the lounge."

They filed, one by one, toward the lounge, as if in a sacred procession.

Large white flakes floated around the large windows of the lounge car. Fina felt like she was in a snow globe. Everyone sat in the same spots as they had last night, as if they'd been directed to do so.

For the first time, Fina laid eyes on the cook. Well, he had to be the cook. He was a barrel-chested man of about forty. He had stubble on his chin which, either by design or accident, suited him. Using a toothpick, he carefully cleaned his teeth.

Laurent removed his cap and clasped his hands together. Bits of his greying hair stood on end, giving him a slightly maniacal appearance. "Ladies and gentlemen. We have an unusual situation..." he trailed off. "Excuse me. Let me first introduce our wonderful cook, Maurice Gaudin." He motioned toward Maurice as if this were an award ceremony.

"Excellent meal, Mr Gaudin," chirped Ada.

"Will you get on with it, please?" whined Dot.

"Yes. *Eh bien,* I am not sure how to explain this, but we had a signal to stop the train immediately. This is why you felt a jolt. While we were waiting for the all-clear signal to continue, an individual boarded the train from the rear – he must have hidden in the tunnel. He made a dash to the front of the train, where he detained the engine driver and his assistant."

Gasps ensued. Eustace gave out a yelp like a hiccough.

"And he's still there?" shrieked Dot.

"Yes," admitted Laurent. "He is on the engine at this moment."

Raoul's face was ashen. "A thief!" he said, twisting the corner of the tablecloth in his long fingers. "You have let a thief on board this train! I must make the strongest protest possible. This person must be caught at once!"

"Did you spy the intruder, or robber, or whoever it was?" asked Etienne. "I assume you did, since you're referring to 'he'."

Laurent shook his head. "But Julien caught a glimpse, *n'est-ce pas*, Julien?"

Julien shrugged. "All that I observed was his back when he was moving through the car. The height is average, not fat, not thin, and he wears a grey suit."

"So we have a well-dressed gentleman robber, is what you're trying to tell us," said Ridgewell.

Laurent shifted his feet and crossed his arms. "It appears that way."

"What does he want? Has he told you? Our valuables? I don't travel with my valuables," said Eustace. "Learned the hard way on Nevis, eh, what?" he said, wheezing at his own private joke.

"*Mon dieu,*" moaned Raoul. "Are the cabins locked?"

"He sent the engine driver back to say he would notify us in due course what the next steps would be," said Julien.

Etienne ran his fingers through his hair and

squinted at his watch. "I must be in Paris by the appointed arrival time of the train. It will be a diplomatic disaster if I snub the Soviet foreign minister."

Sophia said, "And I'm due in Paris for a book signing."

Felix chimed in, "And I, ah, must return for service to my flock." He wouldn't look anyone in the eye. There was something decidedly odd about this priest, Fina thought.

And then a cacophony of voices erupted, all talking over one another about their urgent needs. Fina, Pixley and Ruby glanced at one another with wide eyes.

"What's that noise?" asked Pixley.

"My stomach, you goose," snapped Fina. Yes, she was just as anxious as everyone else about the train robbery, but when her stomach grumbled, all other troubles ebbed away.

"We'd better shovel pieces of toast into Fina, and fast," said Ruby. "I know that look. I'm famished myself. I wonder if Maurice has already made breakfast?"

Pixley padded over to the cook, while everyone continued to chatter around them. Laurent tried several times to calm them all as if they were squabbling schoolchildren. He had little success.

Pixley whispered into Maurice's ear and smiled. He weaved his return through the wildly gesticulating arms of the other passengers.

"We're in luck. Maurice gets up at five o'clock to make breakfast, so it's ready whenever we are."

"Well, what are we waiting for? We're stuck here, so we might as well enjoy a breakfast in the Alps," said Fina.

As they rose, en masse, to be the first ones to escape the chaos of the lounge to the dining car, Ruby grabbed Fina's arm.

"Ow! What's the matter?"

Ruby tapped her teeth, a sure sign that she'd had a breakthrough.

Oh no. There goes breakfast.

"James is missing. Again."

12

James' compartment held no sleeping beauty this time.

He had vanished.

Snowflakes drifted, uninvited, through the half-open window.

"I will check the *toilette* and other cabins," said Laurent.

Ruby nodded her approval. As soon as Laurent moved out of sight, she whispered to Pixley and Fina, "Let's search his cabin. This may be our only chance."

Fina fought back a wave of nausea from hunger. Now she was decidedly cranky. Hands on hips, she said, "We can't do that, it isn't right."

"Maybe not, but neither is spying on us," said Ruby.

Pixley had already begun the search. Fina shrugged. The more quickly this was over, the more quickly she would be at the table gobbling up toast, marmalade, coffee...

"Feens? Can you search the washstand?

The washstand contained nothing unexpected: tooth powder, toothbrush, hair brush, hair cream, Dr Jones' world-famous stomach-settling tonic, half-full bottle of sleeping tonic, and tweezers.

She eyed Pixley, who rifled through James' suitcase. He announced each item: "Passport, Italian banknotes, tennis balls...?"

Pixley peered at Fina and Ruby.

"James is a tennis champion," said Ruby.

Pixley nodded. "Breath mints, one copy of *How to Win at Tennis*, one copy of *Caramel's Revenge* and ... aha!" He held a notebook aloft.

"Quickly – skim it to spot anything of importance," said Ruby.

Pixley pushed his spectacles up the ridge of his nose and plopped down on the bed. He mumbled words as he whispered aloud to himself. "Olbia, Hotel Sardu, Ruby and Fina ... tennis, Milan, tickets ... this is a diary of him following the two of you – and then me, once I joined your party in Sardinia."

Fina shuddered. Pixley looked up. "Yes, it is a disturbing read."

"What about the tickets? We're aware of the other items you mentioned."

"Da da da da…" said Pixley to himself. "Ah! Here it is. Good Lord!"

"Yes?" said Ruby with a sigh. "Do I need to read it for myself or do Fina and I have to play a guessing game?"

"Sorry. It says he planned to steal our tickets to figure out where we were travelling to and then buy tickets to follow us. Ha! See?" said Pixley, grinning. "I wasn't to blame after all for losing the tickets."

"Hmmm…" said Ruby, ignoring Pixley's vindication. She stared at the items she had arranged on the table near the window. She picked up one at a time, replacing each carefully back in its place. A pen, pencil, cigarette case, an empty matchbox, *Baedeker's Guide to Italy*, two ticket stubs to the Milan Opera, and a wrapped boiled sweet.

"Anything of interest?" asked Fina, perusing the table-top items as well.

Ruby sat on the bed next to Pixley. "No, nothing. Other than the notebook Pixley found," she said, turning toward him. "Anything else in there?"

Pixley removed his nose from the notebook. "Here is the entry from November 5th – five days ago. 'I received a disturbing telegram today. They have told me to do something dreadful. I am so upset I don't know what to do. And I am worried that if I don't do what they say, the consequences will be dire. Especially for Mum. I wish she were here. She would tell me what to do. Instead, I'm following two women around Italy like an idiot…'"

Pixley trailed off. "He continues to write about his mother. Poor chap."

A pang of pity hit Fina. James wasn't that bad. He was pathetic. She was certain he hadn't taken up this spying business voluntarily. Besides, when they had discussed the British occupation of New Zealand and treatment of indigenous people like himself – back when they were in Oxford – he had seemed genuine enough. Even if it had been a trap designed to ensnare Fina, given her political commitments.

As Pixley turned another page, a slip of paper fluttered to the floor.

Ruby scooped it up and read aloud. "Selkies and kelpies! It's a receipt for a pistol purchased in Milan!"

Pixley jumped out of his seat like a hen on a hot griddle. He fell to his knees, lifted the blanket on the bed and peered underneath. He shook his head. Then he tried the pillowcase and lifted the mattress. Ruby and Fina joined in and within ten minutes they had turned the entire room upside down.

No pistol. Though they found what seemed to be a lifetime supply of cigarettes. There were so many packets, Fina wondered if James were smuggling them.

"May I ask what are you doing?" queried Laurent from the doorway. His jaw was clenched.

"Oh, ah, we..." stammered Fina.

Pixley intervened. "We saw this receipt for a pistol. A

Beretta 418 with a wooden handle. Small, but deadly. We worried it might be used, accidentally."

Fortunately for the trio, Laurent was under so much strain that the explanation satisfied him. He sighed. "I have asked all the passengers, and no one has seen him since last night. I have searched everywhere – even the galley. Monsieur Matua has well and truly vanished."

"Is it possible that our friend the gentleman thief took him with him to the engine?"

Laurent drew a finger along his jaw. "It's possible, I suppose."

"How will we find out?"

"There's only one way," said Ruby. "We must ask him. The thief, I mean."

"But he said he'd contact us when he's ready. How will we contact him?" asked Fina.

"Well, there's one obvious answer," said Ruby. "I'll knock on the engine door."

"You can't do that!" said everyone in unison.

"Miss Dove, it is certainly too dangerous. As the conductor, I must protest," said Laurent.

Pixley laid a hand on Ruby's arm. "I'll go."

"If this is a misplaced act of male chivalry, Mr Hayford, I won't allow it," said Ruby in a huff.

"I wouldn't do that – at least not intentionally," said Pixley. "I have my reasons. You need to trust me. You can rely on me."

Pixley *had* saved Ruby's and Fina's lives in Sardinia.

"He's right, Ruby," put in Fina. "If he says he has his reasons, we have to believe him."

"Even so," said Laurent, "I cannot allow it." He moved to block the doorway. "I am the captain of this ship. I am the 'law' while we are underway. Especially in an emergency situation."

"We understand, Mr Belrose," said Ruby. "In that case, I'll write a note for you to—" A sudden movement to her left cut her off.

Fina and Ruby gasped.

Pixley held a gleaming, pearl-handled pistol in his hands. Clearly, it wasn't James' pistol. That receipt had been for one with a wooden handle. This one was pointed at the shiny buttons on Laurent's uniform.

Pixley pushed his spectacles up the bridge of his nose with one hand while he held the pistol steady in the other.

"Please do not misunderstand me, Mr Belrose. This is not a threat. It is a friendly suggestion that you let me speak to our gentleman thief."

13

―――――

"Pixley!" cried Ruby. "What are you doing?"

"You have to trust me," he replied without turning around. Laurent moved away from the cabin door, hands held in the air.

Pixley dashed out of the compartment. "I shall return forthwith!"

Ruby offered the shaky conductor a seat. Fina went to the washstand and fetched a glass of water for Laurent, who gulped it down and wiped his brow.

"*La vache*! What is your friend going to do? Why does he assume he and he alone can overcome the thief?"

Ruby shrugged. "Fina and I trust him with our lives. All we can do is wait."

"Can we wait in the dining room?" asked Fina.

Laurent and Ruby stared at Fina in wonder, but they all rose and left the cabin.

In the dining room, everyone else had already tucked into a sumptuous breakfast. Fina's mouth watered as she surveyed plates filled with eggs, sausage, toast, fruit and cheese, all alongside piping-hot pots of tea and coffee.

Fina snapped her napkin open as if she were a professional waiter serving a demanding restaurant. She and Ruby slid into seats next to Sophia and Raoul.

"Ah," sighed Fina as she sipped a cup of coffee with plenty of cream. Sophia smiled. "I agree – I'm much calmer now that I've had coffee and something to eat." Raoul, though, looked as anxious as before. His response to Sophia's comment was to shovel another forkful of eggs into his mouth.

He jabbed his fork in the direction of Ruby. "We saw your friend – Mr Hayford, isn't it? He seemed to be in a rush to go somewhere. I can't imagine why he'd be in a hurry since we have nowhere to go."

Sophia dropped her fork.

Ruby dabbed the corner of her mouth with a napkin. "Yes, well, there's no easy way to say this, so I'll speak plainly. Pixley is going to speak to our gentleman thief – with the hope James Matua is with him."

"Who?"

"James Matua – the passenger from cabin 10. He has

disappeared, it seems." Seeing that Raoul still looked blank, Ruby carried on. "You may not have met him, because he didn't come to the lounge last night. He's a young New Zealander." Her voice faltered. Fina could sympathise with her qualms. A government spy he may have been, but James was still an Oxford student, only in his early twenties – not so different to herself and Ruby.

Raoul stopped chewing and set down his fork. He gave a little bow of his head, as if the information were seeping into his consciousness. "I see. Well, good luck to him is all I can say."

"Sounds foolish," said Sophia, slowly twirling her cup on its saucer.

"Pixley knows what he's doing," said Fina, slamming her cup down on her own saucer with more emphasis than she had intended.

As Laurent passed by their table, Sophia said, "Mr Belrose? Are you able to radio for assistance? Is it possible to have another train sent to rescue us?"

Laurent grimaced. "Yes, I had hoped to do that, but our friend, the thief, has control of all communication. I have access to nothing at the moment."

"But what if another train travels from Genoa in this direction and collides with us?" asked Raoul, eyes opening wide as if the thought only occurred to him as he uttered it.

"Fortunately," replied Laurent, adjusting his cap, "train officials will already realise we are late at this point. We are so late they will delay the other train until they can ascertain the cause. I hope the thief has allowed the engine driver to communicate our position."

"It does seem to be in his own best interest if he keeps away any trains from either direction," said Ruby.

Laurent nodded. "It is the one common interest which we all share."

"I can name another," said Ruby. "Will there be enough provisions to feed us all until the thief decides we can move on? And what about fuel? It's toasty-warm in here at the moment, but I dread to think what would happen if we ran out of coal." She shivered a little as her eyes strayed to the clouds outside, heavy with unfallen snow.

"Mademoiselle, please do not alarm yourself," Laurent said. "The *Train Blanc* carries plentiful supplies of both fuel and food, in case of the avalanche. The engine will continue to warm the carriages. There is no danger." With that, he put down a replacement fork for Sophia, bowed, and moved away toward the next tables.

Seeing that Fina was absorbed in chatting to Ada on her other side, Ruby sipped her tea and turned toward Sophia. "I'm so sorry you'll be late for your author event in Paris. Do you have any other reason you need to be there – another appearance?"

Sophia's eyelid twitched, ever so slightly. "Ah, yes. I will meet with a few author friends and arrange for a few more events while I am there. This was going to be a special event, however," she said, eyes downcast.

"At least we will be able to tour the sights!" said Raoul.

"You haven't been to Paris before?" asked Ruby.

Raoul wiped his mouth. "Always, people believe every French person must have travelled to Paris. All roads lead to Rome, *hein?* No, I am from a small town near the French-Spanish border."

"Is that how you two met?" she asked carelessly.

Sophia turned over her fork on the table in a rhythmic motion. "How did we first meet, Raoul? Ah, I remember! It was at a literary event in Barcelona. That was it. You were a fan and—"

"You asked me to lunch. Then we 'hit it off'. And I have secretarial skills as well." In a deft, conversation-altering move, Raoul cleared his throat to attract Fina's attention. "Now, let me guess your astrological sign, Miss Aubrey-Havelock." He pointed at Ruby. "You are next, Miss Dove."

Before either of them could object – even if they had wanted to – he said, "Miss Aubrey-Havelock. Yes ..." He rubbed his forehead and closed his eyes as if he were predicting the future. "You are a Virgo, Taurus, or even possibly an Aries."

He opened his eyes to see if his choices had hit the mark.

Fina gulped. "How did you know I'm Virgo?"

He smiled. "I can see you are a loyal friend, but you are perhaps also a worrier, *non*?" Fina could only twist her interlocked fingers.

"And now for Miss Dove," he said, repeating the fortune-teller gestures. "Miss Dove is a bit more difficult. Possibly Scorpio because you are passionate, resourceful, and brave ... but no, you are not jealous or violent."

Opening his eyes again, he said, "It isn't coming to me."

"I—" said Ruby.

"Wait!" Raoul exclaimed, holding up a finger. "I have it. You're Aquarius! How stupid I was, but of course. You're forward-thinking, independent, an original, and a humanitarian. But you are also somewhat aloof – to protect yourself – and you dislike emotional expressions. And, how shall I put it, can be a bit uncompromising?"

Fina and Ruby laughed. They laughed so loud that heads turned around the dining car.

"You're quite right, Raoul. I was born on the thirtieth of January. I am most definitely an Aquarian," said Ruby.

14

Pixley strode into the dining car, making a beeline for Laurent. He whispered in Laurent's ear. Laurent clapped him on the back.

Fina let out a sigh of relief. At least one fence had been mended.

Pulling a chair up to their table, Pixley signalled to Julien. "Julien, would you bring me breakfast? The largest breakfast possible. Thank you."

"Well?" said Ruby, tapping her fingers on the linen tablecloth.

"I've spoken to the gentlemen thief and—"

"What does he want?" asked Raoul.

Pixley sniffed. "Do not worry, Mr Lapointe. I will tell you all," he said, shifting in his chair. Ruby poured him a cup of tea.

"The thief has his face covered, so I cannot tell you

his identity. What I can tell you is he is taking good care of the engine driver. He directed the engine driver to communicate to railway officials that we have a technical problem we can repair ourselves. That means, unfortunately, they're not sending anyone to rescue us at the moment."

Everyone's shoulders slumped.

Pixley held up a finger. "However! He has said he will not hold us here indefinitely. And, more importantly, he has no plans to harm us."

"What does he want?" asked Sophia.

"I'm afraid I do not have the answer to that, but I sense it's not money or valuables."

Raoul shrank back into his green suit, so much so it appeared to have become two sizes too large.

"Well, what on earth would he want besides that?" asked Fina.

Ruby scanned the room. "There are several powerful people on the train – such as Etienne and Eustace, even though he's no longer a governor of..." She shuddered.

"You mean he wants to leverage the fact that some of the passengers have influence?" asked Sophia.

"Perhaps," said Ruby. "It seems the most plausible explanation." She took another sip of tea. "I almost forgot – did the thief have James with him?"

"The thief did not have James with him – not that he had any idea who he was in the first place. There are no passengers with him in the engine."

Ruby tapped her teeth.

"I take it the train has been searched," said Sophia, her dangling earrings swaying to and fro.

Fina and Ruby nodded. "Laurent and Julien made a thorough search."

"Well, that leaves only one explanation," said Ruby. "James has left the train."

Pixley motioned to Laurent to join them. This time, instead of looming unsteadily over the table, Laurent pulled up another chair. The other passengers peered curiously at the growing number of people at the table.

Laurent removed his cap, set it on his knee and ran his fingers through his hair. "I know what you are going to ask me. Did James disembark the train during the night?"

Pixley nodded.

"Unfortunately, the answer is no," he said, gesturing toward Julien. "Julien says he passed by James' compartment at five o'clock – the time of our last stop – and heard loud snoring. I believe you are familiar with his snoring," he said, eyeing the trio.

"Yes, it was quite loud," said Ruby. "But can he be sure it wasn't Pixley?"

"Very funny, Ruby," said Pixley. "In all seriousness, though, you're saying James couldn't have left the train after five o'clock because we made no further stops?"

"Yes. So unless James turned on a gramophone

record of his snoring to disguise the fact he'd already left the train, it means he jumped," said Ruby.

"Precisely," said Laurent. "And there certainly isn't any gramophone in his compartment."

Everyone at the table gawked at one another.

Fina said, "Is there a possibility he jumped out when the train was leaving the station at a slow pace?"

Laurent shook his head. "No, this is not possible. You see, when we leave a station, Julien stands near the exit to this sleeping car, and I stand on the exit to the other. Those are the only two exits from the passenger sides of the train. And unless James had found his way to the engine – which is impossible because I would have noticed – he couldn't have jumped off when we were moving slowly out of the station."

"But he could have jumped – or been pushed—"

Sophia reached for her glass of water and knocked it over.

"When the train was at almost full speed," said Ruby, ignoring the minor disturbance.

Laurent nodded. His mouth set in a grim line.

"So – so this means ... that Mr Matua is dead?" squeaked Raoul, voice cracking.

Pixley nodded. "It would seem so. We're not certain if he jumped, or, as Ruby said, was pushed, but it does appear to be the only explanation."

An impromptu moment of silence descended on the table.

Fina stared out of the window at the glowing snow on the peaks opposite them. So peaceful. Such a contrast to the unfolding drama inside these steel boxes.

Laurent rose. "Please excuse me. I'd like to tell the other passengers individually," he said, moving on to the table nearest them.

Sophia said, "The three of you knew Mr Matua. Did he appear suicidal?"

The trio peered at one another. Pixley said, "No, he didn't seem suicidal. But he did look exhausted and worried about something. Besides the fact he was apparently drugged."

"I can imagine what you're thinking," said Ruby, her gaze settling on Sophia. "We were the only ones who knew him, so we are also the only ones who had motives to push him off a moving train."

"I thought no such thing!" exclaimed Sophia. "I thought you might have noticed whether he would do something as drastic as jumping off a moving train."

Ruby was strangely defensive today. Must be the strain. Especially with this new defiant twist to Pixley's personality.

Raoul's eyes lit up. "What if Mr Matua was an acrobat? Or someone like Houdini?! Maybe he had a way of rolling off a speeding train which would leave him unharmed."

All eyes turned toward Raoul. He lowered his eyes to

stare at the salt cellar. "You're right. It is – how do you say in English? Daft."

"Well, what do we do now? Just wait?" asked Sophia. "I do need to finish my writing quota for the day."

As if in answer to her question, Eustace rose from the table next to them, looked around, and cleared his throat.

15

———

"Dear passengers," said Eustace as if he were addressing the House of Lords. "In light of these unfortunate circumstances, we must do whatever is necessary to occupy ourselves – that is, distract ourselves – from our predicament." He adjusted his belt. "And to that end, I propose we begin rounds of cards and other games."

Sophia rolled her eyes. She rose and said, "Thank you, Governor, but I must attend to my writing." She sauntered out of the room. Raoul did not follow. Wasn't a dutiful secretary supposed to follow? Besides, he had been trailing after her like a lost dog for the entire journey. Then Fina realised why Raoul hadn't left. He and Ridgewell had locked eyes from across the room.

Neeya moved toward the door as well. "I must work on a paper due before I arrive in Brussels. Please excuse me."

Ada rose from her seat. "An excellent suggestion, Mr Wistow. I propose a game of poker." Everyone stared at the little old lady in awe.

"That's the spirit!" proclaimed Father Felix, banging his teacup. "I spied chips somewhere in the lounge."

Everyone, save the trio, trundled off in the direction of the lounge.

"Shall we join them?" asked Fina.

"Yes," whispered Ruby. "But not before we've done a little snooping."

"What? Snooping? At a time like this? Why?" asked Fina.

"I can tell Ruby and I are on the same page," said Pixley. "We both believe James didn't jump – someone pushed him."

"But what would be the reason? As Sophia and Raoul pointed out, we're the only ones with a motive."

"It's true," replied Ruby. "But there are too many coincidences on this journey. First James, then these powerful and not-so-powerful people with secrets. Finally, we have the so-called thief who has no desire to do any thieving."

Pixley nodded. "We ought to search any of the cars which are empty. Fortunately for us, Julien and Laurent are busy helping Maurice or attending to the other passengers in the lounge."

"And I'm keen on chatting with Neeya as well," said Ruby.

THE FIRST COMPARTMENT they came to was number 1. Father Felix Schweinsteiger's cabin. Pixley stood guard in the hallway. He had also procured a skeleton key from Laurent. Fina didn't ask him how he came by it.

Everything was orderly. A Bible sat on the ledge near the window. His modest wardrobe was neat and pressed. Even his toothbrush, hairbrush and tooth powder were lined up with precision. An empty chocolate box also stood on the ledge.

Ruby stuck her hand underneath his pillow. "Aha! Works like a charm," she said, pulling out a wad of papers. They were receipts for ordinary expenditures, such as a hotel, restaurant, museum, and the like. Nothing out of the ordinary.

"Why stow receipts under his pillow?" asked Fina.

Ruby shrugged.

They finished their search under the bed and through his empty suitcase. Nothing of interest, other than an address book. The names in the address book were German or Italian, and largely unremarkable.

Fina felt deflated as they left the cabin. At least Father Felix was no longer a suspect.

Ruby smiled. "Every time we find a perfectly ordinary cabin, we can eliminate them as a suspect."

"Except if they're *too* ordinary, if you know what I mean," said Pixley.

"True. Especially since they might be carrying around any items of interest – knowing the conductor might search their cabin," replied Ruby. "We'll keep that in mind."

"Who's next on our list?"

"Ridgewell," replied Pixley as he unlocked cabin number 3.

"He seems to be a quiet sort of cove," said Pixley. "Let's see if still waters run deep."

Unlike Father Schweinsteiger's compartment, Ridgewell's was a comparative mess. What was odd, though, was that Ridgewell had very few belongings. It was as if someone had already searched his compartment.

One thing he did have was a love of hats. Fedoras, walkers, bowlers, homburgs, and boat hats. They hung from every available spot in the cabin, giving it the effect of a haberdashery. He also enjoyed colourful scarves, which were strewn around the hats. Despite the disorder, Fina liked Ridgewell – at least the personality conveyed by his room. It seemed still waters did run deep.

Pixley's head appeared in the doorway. "Someone's coming!"

Ruby and Fina crouched down in a recess by the washstand. Pixley shut the door. They heard murmurs outside.

"Have you seen Mr Synge?"

"Mmmm, no, Mr Lapointe, I was looking for him myself. He's not in his cabin. Better have a look in the lounge. I'll catch you up in a moment. Must tie my shoes."

Footsteps faded.

Ruby and Fina let out the air they held in their lungs.

"All clear," whispered Pixley through the door. "Look lively, girls!"

Ruby had already searched half the room, with little to show. They redoubled their efforts.

"Bingo!" she said, holding up two passports. They were both British.

"Uh, why does he have two passports?" asked Fina.

"That's what I'd like to know," said Ruby, flipping through them. "One is for Ridgewell Synge, the other for Ridgewell Hinton. Other than that, they're identical."

"Perhaps he's changed his name, so he carries both passports at once? Just in case there are any difficulties at the border?"

"Good point," said Ruby. "I hadn't considered that. Either way, it won't be easy to ask him."

A large sketchbook was balanced on a trunk. "Look!" Fina said, flipping through the pages filled with charcoal drawings. "Aren't they marvellous?"

"Beautiful. Real talent," replied Ruby, taking the pad. "He's already drawn most of the passengers. Though a few sheets have been torn out."

"Who's missing?" asked Fina.

"Well, it's not that they're missing – because we've only been on the train a short time. He may not have had time to sketch us all. Neeya, Eustace, Sophia, Raoul, Dot and Ada are missing."

"Who would want to draw a portrait of Dot anyway?" giggled Fina. "Besides, he spends a great deal of time with her."

"It's true," said Ruby. "Which is why it's curious there are so many drawings of his mother. Though she is a lovely woman."

"Are there any sketches of us?"

Ruby gave out a great belly laugh. "He's definitely captured Pixley. See?" she said, handing the pad over to Fina.

Pixley sat scribbling furiously in his notebook while twirling his spectacles. "His sketch of you is quite accurate as well, Ruby," said Fina as she flipped to the next page. Ruby was shown in an impeccable outfit, gazing out of the train carriage window. She was clearly deep in thought.

Fina laughed at herself. The next page was a drawing of Fina enjoying a slice of cake. "He's certainly caught the essence of our personalities."

"Let's not become too side-tracked. Is there anything else?" asked Ruby.

Fina shook her head. "A few books, including one by Sophia Salazar."

"I must read one of her books," said Ruby. "It certainly seems to be the fashionable thing to do."

A knock came from the door. Pixley popped his head in. "Someone's coming. Hurry!"

16

There was just time for Ruby and Fina to slip out into the corridor. They dived into an intent conversation.

Neeya approached, book in hand.

"Ah, Neeya! Just the person I wanted to talk to," said Ruby. She winked at Pixley and Fina. "Would you mind if we returned to your compartment to discuss something?" she asked, turning back to Neeya.

"Of course. I finished writing the draft of my paper, so I have nothing in particular to do. Especially as we aren't travelling anywhere for the foreseeable future."

Ruby followed Neeya to her cabin.

After Neeya offered Ruby a chocolate – which Ruby refused – they settled down on the sofa.

"What would you like to discuss?"

"The reason I wanted to discuss this with you alone was to avoid any embarrassment or awkwardness on my part," said Ruby. "As I believe I already mentioned to you, I'm a dress designer – Fina is my assistant. I immediately noticed what lovely clothes you had."

Neeya's eyes glowed with appreciation. "Thank you. A love of clothes is scoffed at, I'm afraid, in the academic world. Especially since I'm a woman – it's considered frivolous and not serious enough. But I cannot help it. I enjoy it."

"I agree," shuddered Ruby. "Even as an undergraduate, I can imagine that happening at Oxford." She fingered the embroidered hem of a skirt draped across the arm of the sofa. "So, now to the awkward part of the conversation," she continued. "You have such beautiful clothes – and clearly an eye about how to select them – but the pieces you wear together don't necessarily always ..."

"Seem as if they ought to be worn together?" Neeya finished the sentence.

Ruby sighed. "Precisely."

Neeya smiled. "No need to feel awkward about it. I'm glad you noticed. I have an eye for what looks sharp on others, but not on myself. Which is why I can select beautiful pieces but am hopeless when I want to create an ensemble."

"Having an eye is what matters – which is what you have. From there, it's simple to give you a few pointers," said Ruby. She stood up and began to rearrange the hangers with Neeya's clothes.

When they had finished the first lesson, Neeya said, "I sense I can trust you, Ruby. I see you're a kind and brave person. And also one with a brain, which is something I admire."

Ruby grinned. "That's one of the nicest things anyone has ever said to me. Thank you, Neeya. I have to admit I noticed something was on your mind, though I obviously couldn't know the source of your preoccupation."

Neeya's lip quivered but then held fast. "I haven't told this to anyone, so please keep it to yourself – or at least to Pixley and Fina, since you trust them."

"Go on," said Ruby.

For the second time that morning, Ruby jumped at the sight of a gun. Neeya's tiny, wooden-handled pistol had been hidden underneath her pillow, and now it waved loosely in Neeya's hand.

"For God's sake, don't point it at me, Neeya!" yelped Ruby as she pushed the gun away from her.

"Oh!" Neeya held a hand over her mouth. "I'm so sorry. I've never handled a gun before."

"You'd better give that to me," said Ruby, slipping the toy-like pistol into her clutch. "I'll see to it. Don't worry," she said, smoothing her hair and skirt. "Now, tell me, step by step, how you came to possess this weapon."

Neeya's hands curled into a ball on her lap. As soon as they had settled there, they flew up as she began her tale. "I'm afraid I didn't sleep well last night. The bed was comfortable, but I usually jerk awake whenever the train comes to a halt. I have a rather bad habit of checking the time when I awake. It's a bad habit because I either despair as to how many more hours of fitful sleep lie ahead, or else I realise it's almost time to wake up."

Ruby sat patiently through this detailed description of her sleeping habits.

"I'll return to my story. I awoke when we stopped in Domodossola at five o'clock. Then I awoke again forty-five minutes later. I heard shuffling in the corridor and a heavy thud. Then silence. The thud was so loud that I slipped out of bed and peeked into the corridor."

"And that's when you noticed the gun on the floor," said Ruby.

"Exactly. There was no one in the corridor, so I picked it up. Needless to say, I didn't sleep for the rest of the night."

"It would be difficult to do so. Is there a reason you didn't report it to the conductor?"

"I was going to, but then James disappeared, and I thought it would seem awkward that I had suddenly found a pistol – even though James apparently jumped. And we would have heard a gunshot had it gone off inside the train."

"So why are you telling me this now?" asked Ruby.

"I'm a keen observer of others. That's how I managed to pass the law exam in Cairo. I learn what is expected of me and how to adapt through observation. I had an immediate sense you were someone who could figure out what was going on. And our little discussion proved I could trust you."

A tap came at the door.

"Ruby? Are you in there?"

Fina popped her head around the doorframe.

"Pixley and I thought you two might have fallen asleep in here, you've been so long. Let's go to the lounge. Ada told us they're going to start a round of charades."

"But you hate charades, Fina," said Ruby.

Neeya laughed, along with Pixley, who had also popped in.

"Well, yes, that's quite right. But I enjoy watching them."

"It will be a welcome distraction, I suppose," said Ruby. "Though like Fina, I refuse to participate."

"Where's your spirit of adventure, Ruby?" grinned Pixley.

"I imagine you're a dab hand at charades, aren't you, Pixley?" asked Fina.

"Well ... I have been known to win a few rounds," he said with his best innocent look.

CHARADES WERE WELL UNDERWAY in the lounge. And

with a little help from early cocktails, Fina noticed. Why not start early? It was probably the best way to cope with the situation, though she knew it could go too far.

"Something to drink, Miss Aubrey-'avelock?" asked Julien, clearly reading her mind.

"Well, it's a little early for me..." said Fina.

"Perhaps, but under this circumstance, I would counsel you to take at least one alcoholic beverage. For – 'ow you say – medicinal purposes only, of course," he grinned.

"In that case, I'll take a gin and tonic."

"I'll have a sidecar, please, Mr Paquet," said Ruby.

"Scotch for me," said Pixley.

"Black coffee for me," said Neeya.

Ada and Felix still played a feverish game of cards. Sophia had returned, though she scribbled in a note-book in the corner. Everyone else was engrossed in charades. Eustace was enjoying himself immensely as he wagged his finger and stamped his foot.

"Argument!"

"Stubborn!"

"Certainty. To be sure." At those words, the governor brightened and looked encouraging.

"Shirley Temple!" yelled Dot with childlike abandon.

The governor wavered and signalled he was moving to the next part.

He pulled at his hair. What was left of it.

"Sure Hair?" laughed Ridgewell.

"Lock?" queried Pixley.

The governor pointed at Pixley.

"Sherlock Holmes!" cried Pixley. Applause all around.

"Now it's your turn, Mr Hayford," said Mrs Synge.

Pixley took a sip of his scotch, removed his jacket and moved into the centre of the carriage. He adjusted his clothing as if he were preparing for a game of cricket. Then he flapped his arms.

"A bird!" yelled Raoul.

Pixley ignored him and kept flapping, lifting himself on his tiptoes so it appeared he was launching into space. Then he snapped his wings shut and cowered as if afraid of something, pulled out his handkerchief and wiped his brow.

Silence.

"A scared bird?" said Madeline.

"Don't be ridiculous, Mother," said Dot.

Pixley pointed at a candle on the table.

"I know!" exclaimed Ruby in a fit of unusual enthusiasm. "Icarus!"

Pixley smiled and bowed, to thunderous applause.

When the applause died down, Fina spotted a figure slumped over her chair.

Neeya.

17

Eustace, who sat next to Neeya, felt for her pulse.

"Good gracious!" cried Dot, always the first to exclaim at anything untoward. "Is she all right? What happened?"

Eustace didn't reply. He kept one hand on Neeya's wrist and the other on his watch, which he had pulled from his waistcoat pocket. The silence seemed to stretch on interminably.

"*Governor*," said Madeline, her voice lower than her daughter's, but insistent.

Eustace's pasty pale jowls shook, signalling a negative result.

A surge of acid rage spewed up from Fina's stomach. Before the charades, Neeya had clearly changed into a Ruby-approved ensemble, making the scene even more tragic somehow. She was so brave and brilliant. Fina hadn't realised it until this moment but Neeya had been an inspiration to her.

And now all that remained was a lifeless, limp body sprawled across the table.

Ruby approached Neeya, bending down to sniff her cup of coffee. She stiffened. "Cyanide."

Fina's eyes fixed on each passenger, one by one. She would have her revenge on whoever had done this. And she would discover the murderer before Ruby.

Despite the passengers' remarkably different personalities, all wore similar looks of shock. But Fina knew one of them – at least one of them – was pretending.

Then, like the calm before a storm, everyone erupted into nervous chatter which crescendoed into exclamations.

"But – but who would do such a thing?" cried Madeline.

"The work of the *Teufel*," said Ada, shaking her head.

"Yes, the devil has a hand in this, Mrs Hartman," said Felix.

"The devil can go to hell," said Raoul. "One of us did it. A real, live person."

Heads bobbed in agreement.

Laurent stood up and adjusted his uniform. "Ladies and gentlemen, as the acting arm of the law on this train, I am afraid I will need to search your persons."

"But surely it was an accident," wailed Dot.

Ridgewell stared at his sister but said nothing.

Pixley said, "Quite right, Mr Belrose. How are we going to search the ladies, though?"

"I nominate Mrs Hartman for the task," said Ruby.

"Very well," said Laurent, peering at Ada. "Do you agree, Mrs Hartman?"

"Yes, *Schätze*," she said as her bun quivered. "But what ought I to search for? After all, if cyanide capsules killed her, there would be no sign of that unless the murderer was stupid enough to carry an entire box."

Etienne nodded. "Mrs Hartman is correct. Why would a murderer keep a box on his or her person? All he or she would need to do is pop the pill into the coffee cup."

Laurent paused, removed his cap, and ran his hands through his hair. "What you say, Mrs Hartman and Mr Durand, is true. Nevertheless, I still believe a search is in order."

"Stubborn old so-and-so, isn't he?" whispered Eustace to Fina. A strong odour of scotch wafted from his moustache. Fina didn't respond.

Laurent nodded to Julien and Maurice, who stood in the rear of the lounge. They carried Neeya quietly and efficiently away, to somewhere near the front of the train.

Julien returned and, under Laurent's direction, began to search the passengers.

Ada stood up, launching her ball of yarn onto the

floor. "*Ach du liebe Zeit,*" she said as Ruby retrieved the yarn. She smiled and patted Ruby on the arm.

The women trailed after Ada to the back of the lounge. Ada's friendly expression never wavered. Her eyes twinkled even as she examined the women's clothes for pockets. What was it about this woman? There was something about the old dear that she was missing – some crucial piece of information that Ada had let slip, unnoticed.

Fina's musings were interrupted by a shout from the other end of the carriage. "*Mon Dieu!*" exclaimed Julien, holding a small enamelled box aloft. "Cyanide pills!"

Ridgewell blubbered, "But – I – it's not possible! I wasn't even aware cyanide came in capsules, much less where to get it! Someone planted it on me!"

Madeline rushed to her son. "Don't worry, Wellie. I'm sure there's an explanation," she said, glaring at Laurent like a mother bear staring down an approaching hunter.

Laurent shrugged. "It may be, it may not be. Let us continue the search."

"But you just found the murderer!" exclaimed Eustace. "Don't be stubborn, man."

"Too right, Governor," echoed Dot from the other end of the lounge.

Raoul stepped forward, his shoulders tense. "I, too, agree. This searching must stop! Ah, no, I refuse – no one must search anymore!"

Laurent ignored the outbursts. "Please, do continue," he said, waving his hand. Raoul stepped back, defeated, grimacing in frustration.

Ada's surprisingly agile fingers had made rapid searches of the women. She instructed them to empty their handbags on small tables arranged around the room. Though inspecting these items was a mammoth task for anyone, Ada attacked it with relish.

Ruby was the last to open her clutch. She pursed her lips and said to Ada, "Before I open this, I ought to tell you I have a pistol inside."

Though Ruby uttered the word 'pistol' quietly, all heads in the room turned.

Ruby held it aloft in her palm after emptying the contents of her clutch onto the table.

Pixley said, "I'm sure Ruby will share with us why she has a pistol, but it seems irrelevant as Miss Arafa was poisoned. After all, I have a pistol myself."

"Excellent point, Mr Hayford, but I would like to know why Miss Dove has a pistol," said Laurent.

Everyone reconvened in the centre of the lounge. Ruby told her story of how the wooden-handled pistol, originally James's, came to be in her possession.

"Thank you, Miss Dove. The story rings true precisely because it's all so far-fetched," said Laurent. He turned to Ruby and Pixley. "I will need to take your weapons from you for safekeeping, however, in light of recent events." Ruby and Pixley looked at each other, shrugged, and complied. "And I request that anyone else who has a weapon with them hand it over immediately," he said, turning slowly around the room. No one responded to his offer.

Etienne shook his head. "None of this makes any sense. First Mr Matua jumps – or was pushed – off the train after leaving a pistol in the hallway. Miss Arafa retrieves it and then she is murdered."

Ridgewell squeaked, "And don't forget the murderer tried to pin the crime on me!"

Etienne's eyes narrowed. "Be that as it may. I agree it is preposterous, but it might be a clever double-bluff."

Dot cleared her throat. "It's obvious. Mr Matua was killed for an unknown reason. But Miss Arafa saw the pistol. She may have seen something else without realising it – something incriminating. Perhaps she had to die because the murderer thought she knew something – because she had the gun."

Fina blinked at Dot, reappraising this irritating soul. She had a brain, after all. Too bad it took a murder for her to display its qualities.

Etienne said, assuming the role of leader he was accustomed to playing, "I suggest, Mr Belrose, you tell our gentleman thief what has happened. It might make him reconsider his position if a murder has occurred on the train."

"It might make the man turn violent," said Madeline.

"Or it might make him decide to exit the train and be rid of us," said Felix. "I'm sure he didn't bargain for a murder when he boarded our train."

Laurent rubbed his chin. "*Oui*," he said, slapping his thighs with determination. "I will do it. Or, I ought to say, I request Mr Hayford communicate with him – since you seem to have a special bond."

"A special bond! How do we know that man is not conspiring with the thief!" exclaimed Eustace.

Pixley cleaned his spectacles. "You don't know, but I suspect the only way we'll escape this mare's nest is for me to speak to him."

18

"My head is spinning," whined Fina, as she and Ruby settled themselves back in their compartment.

"Mine, too. It's difficult enough to understand our captive train situation without having the addition of murder," sighed Ruby. She padded to the washstand and splashed water on her face. "That's better," she said, patting her skin dry. "I'm hopeful Pixley will accomplish something."

Fina's anxious, worried mind had completely taken over her consciousness. "But how are we going to get out of this disaster, even if we are rescued? Pixley is implicated in some way – even if he's not, he threatened a train conductor with a gun! And you were found with a pistol in your clutch. And..."

Ruby gave Fina's hand a squeeze. "It will all turn out fine, Feens. Remember how many times we've been in a seemingly hopeless situation over the past year? It's more than an average person would have in a lifetime! But we're still alive, and intellectually and emotionally intact. Well, mostly."

At those words, Fina's mind turned to her brother and her father. Her father's murder, her brother's execution. It was all too much. And they still hadn't vindicated her brother, Connor. She glanced at Ruby. "But my family. The murder..." She trailed off.

"This isn't like you, Fina Aubrey-Havelock," said Ruby. "The Fina I know is, well, yes, a bit anxious, but also as firm as the base of a tree." She paused for a sip of water. "I know what will take your mind off the past! Let's write down everything we've learned. It will help us empty our minds. I always feel better after we've done this exercise in the past."

"You're too good to me, Miss Dove," smiled Fina, wiping away incipient tears. She sniffed. "Yes, let's do it. I have a stack of stiff notecards in my suitcase. We can use those for each passenger."

"Let's scribble away, Sherlock!" declared Ruby. Fina smiled, knowing no response was needed. She was definitely Watson, though she considered her brain power to be a cut above the good doctor's. And she could throw a punch as confidently as he could, too.

"I'll start with the victims," said Fina. She wrote 'James Matua' on a card and then flipped it over to fill in the details.

"James Matua," said Ruby, rising from the bed. Her pacing was limited to awkward half-circles, given the layout of the cabin. "We are certain he is a willing or unwilling spy for the British government, against us. Ian warned us about him, so it's logical that other people are aware he is a spy."

"Especially because he gave himself away to us – the very people he was following," said Fina. "I still can't believe he had the nerve to show up when we were in Sardinia."

"Precisely. His ineptitude shows a lack of will. The government must have forced him to spy, rather than enticed him to do so."

"He might have been in training," said Fina.

"True. Although poor James would need a lot more training." She paused, tapping her teeth. "But I must give him his due. He followed us all the way to Sardinia, then Milan, and then to this train."

"We also know he purchased a pistol in Milan and brought it with him on the train."

"Yes, it is odd. Why would he buy a pistol in Milan? If he had bought it for general protection, surely he would have brought it with him when he left England."

"That means he either lost the pistol he had brought with him – an entirely likely scenario since he was so clumsy – or circumstances changed."

"Let's assume your second point is the valid one for now. Circumstances changed. Which circumstances?"

"Either he was in danger, or—" Fina gulped.

"Yes, or he was going to use it for nefarious purposes," finished Ruby.

"Don't forget that telegram he received. It ordered him to do 'something dreadful'."

The two women exchanged a look. Neither wanted to speculate on what that something might have been.

"What about the tainted chocolates? Why was he drugged?" asked Fina.

"It must have something to do with the purchase of the pistol."

"What about the thief? Maybe he inserted sleeping powder into the chocolates?"

"This is getting rather fantastical now," said Ruby, sighing. "But I have to admit our present scenario is rather fantastical itself." She shook her head. "I cannot comprehend how our thief might have tampered with the chocolates. The thief would have no way of knowing which box would go to which cabin. He also couldn't have boarded the train in Genoa without Laurent or Julien noticing. No, it must have been a passenger."

"Yes, the other passengers. How about Neeya?" said Fina as her shoulders slumped.

Ruby flopped down on the bed. "I didn't know her but for a few hours but she was one of us, Feens."

"I feel the same way," said Fina, anger rising in her voice. "Which is why we must solve the murder, in her memory. What we've gathered about her is this: she was the first woman to earn a law degree in Egypt. Could a disgruntled male colleague be pursuing a vendetta? Seems implausible."

"I agree, but write it down anyway," said Ruby. "She was travelling to Brussels to begin her PhD course. We're familiar with academic quarrels, but would someone really go so far as to track her down and kill her with cyanide on the *Train Blanc*? There aren't any academic types on the train – other than us."

"A jealous lover?" suggested Fina. "Yes, no need to tell me it's implausible – but I'll write it down anyway."

"How about a political angle?" said Ruby.

"Hmmm... you mean she's like us – or works for a government? We do have two people involved in high levels of government," said Fina. "Do you think she was involved in Egyptian politics?

"It's a definite possibility, but it seems unlikely. Remember how the British foreign secretary told the Egyptians that their more progressive 1923 constitution was 'unworkable'?"

"Did he?"

"That prompted the massive student protests over the past month or so against the current British-backed government. Since Neeya is young – and a student – she would either still be in Egypt because of the protests, or she would have mentioned them to me if she were somehow involved or supportive of them. I was waiting for her to say something about it, but she didn't."

"Makes sense. So she is what she says she is. A student about to begin another round of studies in Belgium."

Ruby nodded. "Now, what about the rest of the passengers?"

"Governor Eustace Wistow. Former governor of Leeward Islands," said Fina.

Ruby shuddered. "Curious. Too much of a coincidence we're both on the train, don't you think?"

"Was he the governor at the time of the massacre? The one with Lieutenant Trace, that we uncovered at Pauncefort?"

Ruby shook her head. "No, he was the governor just before that. But he's still responsible for supporting those conditions," she said with venom. Fina's mind cast back to their first case at Pauncefort Hall and the details of Lieutenant Trace's testimonial letter they had found. St Kitts plantation owners had murdered ten sugarcane workers. And the government had covered it up. She ground her teeth at the memory of it, especially the look on Ruby's face when they had found the document during their snowbound weekend with a murderer on the loose.

"It's amazing – these people seem like bumbling old grandfathers, don't they? Not particularly nice, but not particularly offensive, either," said Fina.

"I agree. This one likes to be the centre of attention –

no surprise there – and likes to be the life of the party. Other than that, we have little information about him."

"I wish we could search his compartment," said Fina, leaning against the wall as she wrote. "Etienne Durand? He's a French diplomat involved in high-level talks with the Soviets. Tight-lipped about his personal life."

"Yes, no apparent motive. How about our friend the priest?"

"Felix Schweinsteiger. Swiss German. Collector of receipts and—"

"Likes card games," finished Ruby. "Very much. Remember how eager he was to play poker last night?"

"He almost leapt off his chair when it was suggested. And did you see how much he bet?"

"Why, no, I wasn't looking. Was it a lot?"

"Heaps," said Fina. "For a priest."

"Where does he get that kind of money? And even more implausibly, where does he get the money to take *Train Blanc*?"

"I hadn't thought of that," said Fina, scribbling rapidly. "Very suspicious, but no connection to James or Neeya. And neither of them had money."

"I'm not so sure about Neeya," said Ruby. "Remember, she had those lovely clothes. And she was taking the *Train Blanc* as well. Does that mean her family has a great deal of money?"

"Mmmhh," said Fina. "What about our sultry writer and her young Casanova?"

"I've not heard anything against them. They seem completely taken up with spreading the word about Sophia's salacious stories." Ruby's lips twitched. "I wonder if the books will take Paris by storm?"

"Ooh la la!" said Fina, giggling. "As will the pair of them!"

"Raoul told me he was keen to see the sights of Paris, but it's a fair bet that Paris will be just as keen to see him, with those looks."

Fina swivelled to face her friend. "He told you he was keen to see Paris?" she breathed with rising excitement.

"Yes, just yesterday – what is it?"

Wide-eyed, Fina tapped her pen against her teeth. "When I was chatting to Etienne after dinner last night, I asked him if he knew where Raoul was from in France. It was an inane question that popped into my head since I had nothing else to say to Etienne."

"And?"

"Etienne said he had trouble identifying the accent but later told me it was Parisian."

Ruby's eyebrows lifted. "So! Raoul is definitely lying. He's either from Paris and pretending he's never been there—"

"Or it's a fake Parisian accent. That would explain

why it was difficult for Etienne to identify it in the first place."

"Intriguing. And promising."

"What about her?" asked Fina.

"She's hiding something, too. I'm sure of it. Though I haven't a clue what it is. As a controversial author, perhaps she's used to hiding unimportant trivialities. Maybe it's second nature to her."

"No doubt. How about the ghastly Synge clan?" Fina caught herself. "That's unfair – it's really only Dot that's ghastly. But who are they and where are they from? What do they do? Are they simply upper-class aristocratic spongers?"

"Well, to be honest, that's what I assumed," said Ruby. "In my mind, they belong to the Riviera set – not fabulously wealthy, but wealthy enough to travel."

"Maybe the absent father left them a fortune. Unless there was some scandalous divorce."

"Madeline seems to be falling for Sophia, and Ridgewell for Raoul. But that all developed on board the train and has no obvious connection to the murders. Except, of course, those pills found on Ridgewell. Though I don't think he had anything to do with the murder at all. Someone planted them on him."

"Now, we come to your friend, Ada."

Ruby's eyes softened. "Yes, she is a character, as they say. Tough as nails and sweet as sugar. That woman certainly has a past, though I have no idea what it is."

"She's a fiend for cards," said Fina. "Much like Father Schweinsteiger."

"But unlike him, I get the feeling she wins at it regularly. She's no fool, our little old grandma," giggled Ruby.

"And yet she doesn't seem to be hiding anything. In fact, she's remarkably frank. She told me…" And then it hit Fina like a runaway train. *Braunschweig.* Brunswick in English. That was where Ada had said she was from – the town where the National Socialists had a training school. She had read about it in the newspaper. It had made the British government nervous.

Could the affable Frau Hartman be harbouring a secret even more sinister than they'd thought possible?

Looking out of the window at the snow-capped peaks, Fina shivered. It seemed unthinkable that such a malign influence could be at work on their cosy train. She decided not to mention the connection to Ruby – not yet, anyway. Luckily, Ruby hadn't noticed that she'd never finished her thought about Ada.

"Finally, we come to the staff," she resumed. "Laurent? Julien? Maurice?"

"I suppose any of them might have done it. They'd have an excuse to be wandering the corridors. They'd also have excellent opportunity to slip cyanide into Neeya's coffee."

"But no apparent motives. Unless one of them is involved in political intrigue, which seems unlikely.

None of them appears to have been hired only for this train journey. They are all professional."

Before she could go any further, the door burst open and Pixley leaned into the cabin. "I have news."

Mopping his head, he tumbled onto the bed. Fina reseated herself in the one chair in the cabin.

He hunched over his legs, head bent down. Staying in the same position, he lifted his head. His mouth was pulled down at the corners. Grave. That's was the only way to describe his countenance. Fina had never seen this version of Pixley. He certainly hid his other, more serious side well. But that wasn't fair to him. He'd been perfectly serious in the past. No, she reflected, this side had been there before – she just hadn't noticed it. Her mind had fixed on one idea of Pixley and had been unwilling to appreciate him in all of his complexity. After all, he had saved their lives in Sardinia.

Ruby patted Pixley on the shoulder. "There's no rush, Pixley. Take whatever time you need."

He glanced at her with a wan smile. "Thanks, Ruby. To be honest, I'm feeling a little queasy."

Fina leapt up. "I have ginger sweets. They always help me – the worst they can do is not have an effect," she said, retrieving them from her sponge-bag on the washstand.

Pixley sucked on the ginger lozenge. After the third one, he had perked up considerably. Fina smiled. She knew the sugar would make him chirpy as a starling.

"So, I can guess your news: you've come to tell us the identity of the gentleman thief, haven't you?" said Ruby, the ghost of a smile on her lips.

Fina gaped. "His identity! But Ruby, how can you possibly—"

Pixley was speechless so Ruby turned to Fina. Smoothing her hair, she announced, "No need to worry, dearest. This gentlemen thief, over whom so many people on this train have lost so much sleep, is none other than Mr Ian Clavering, theatre producer, and snooper extraordinaire."

19

Fina fell out of her chair. "Ouch," she said, as Ruby helped her up. "Excuse me? What do you mean, the thief is Ian? Is there some other Ian Clavering in existence?"

Pixley removed his glasses and put them back on to stare at Ruby. "How the devil did you know? Are you a psychic in all your spare time, Miss Ruby Dove?"

Ruby didn't smile but Fina could tell by the way the corners of her eyes crinkled that she was enjoying herself. "Before you ask, I didn't receive a letter from Ian telling me he would take *Train Blanc* captive. But it was the combination of two things that gave it away. First, he sent us the train tickets. Second, Pixley was obviously familiar with the thief."

"Ian will be furious you figured it out," said Pixley,

laughing and holding one cupped hand up to his mouth.

"Well, he ought to know better than to underestimate me by now," she said with a little huff.

"Admit, it, Ruby," gasped Fina, laughing so hard now that the tears rolled down her cheeks, "You are pleased as punch now he's here."

"I'll admit no such thing. The man is a complete and utter fool. To believe he can hold a train full of passengers hostage – *Train Blanc*, no less – and get away with it, is the height of arrogance."

"So that's why he insisted on us having the last carriages in the train. Pixley, you welcomed him in, you old devil! I cannot believe I'm laughing," said Fina, as she continued to giggle. "But the whole situation is utterly absurd!"

"I do not find it very humorous," Ruby said, looking askance at Pixley and Fina. "And I cannot understand why you two find it funny in the least."

Pixley and Fina glanced at each other and suppressed further laughter. "You're quite right, Ruby," said Pixley, trying his best to wipe a grin off his face.

"Is Laurent aware we know who it is?"

He shook his head. "I still haven't told him. But Ian said to give his love to you and Fina."

"Pshiah," said Ruby. "The man is a fool."

"That may be," said Pixley, "But you must admit he's fantastically brave."

"Like a suicidal maniac is brave," Ruby retorted.

"There's time enough to discuss Ian later," said Fina. "Now, what did you tell Laurent? Word for word, please."

"I told him Ian ordered a thorough search of all of the compartments and a detailed, itemised list of everything in those compartments. Ian said he would consider his next steps after that. I told Laurent the thief wanted to resolve this as quickly as possible."

"The search will take ages!" said Fina.

"Laurent, Julien and Maurice have already begun. I expect they'll need assistance preparing food since Maurice is helping with the search."

Fina's stomach rumbled. "We can help – what else do we have to do?"

"But wait," said Ruby. "The most important question hasn't been answered yet. Why has Ian taken us as captives?"

"Good question," said Pixley. "On the day we departed Sardinia, I received a letter similar to Ruby's. He directed me to take this train with you two. I also received a coded message later. The message hinted something would occur on the train. It also said I should prepare to do whatever was necessary to 'make contact'. I didn't understand what it meant at the time. But as soon as the train was held hostage, it made sense."

"So you're saying you don't know his reasons for doing it?" asked Fina.

Pixley nodded. "I cajoled him in every way I knew how. But you know how stubborn he can be. Like you two," he finished.

"Stubborn?" said Ruby and Fina in outrage.

"Not us, certainly not us," said Fina with finality.

"Be that as it may," said Pixley, rolling his eyes ever so slightly, "I have no idea what he's playing at. Honestly," he said, laying his hand over his heart.

"Do you think we can read the detailed list before you give it to Ian?" asked Ruby.

"Ian said Laurent should show the list to everyone to see if it helps anyone figure out who the murderer might be."

Fina peered at her watch. "It's well past one o'clock. Shall we ask Maurice if we can help in the galley?"

They strolled down the hallway. Sophia and Raoul's cabin doors were shut. Fina smiled as she put her ear to Raoul's door. She could make out the contented purr of a cat. All she could hear at Sophia's door was light humming. Or was it a soft crying?

In the second sleeping carriage, Ruby held up one finger and stopped.

"Oof," said Fina as she bumped into her.

"Shhh..." whispered Ruby, pointing to Mrs Synge's compartment. The door was open just a crack.

"Well, this puts us in a rather difficult position," came the voice of Mrs Synge.

"Everything's a shambles," said Dot. Her voice

sounded odd. Fina replayed her words over in her head until it hit her: the particular whingeing quality that had characterised Dot's conversation all through the journey was missing.

"Do you think they'll find out?" asked Ridgewell.

"Not if you keep your cool," said Mrs Synge.

"Well, I'm off to Bedfordshire," said Ridgewell. "At least for an hour's nap. I'm all in."

"Oh Ridgewell, you could sleep for England!"

Footsteps approached. Presumably Ridgewell's.

Ruby and Fina strolled toward the front of the train, but not soon enough.

The door to the compartment popped open. "Hullo," said Ridgewell with a smirk. "Doing a bit of eavesdropping, I see." He crossed his arms, clearly waiting for an explanation.

"Oh – I – ah – we..." stammered Fina.

"I can see how this looks, Mr Synge," said Ruby, waving her arms apologetically. "We were on our way to see if Maurice needed assistance with preparing our next meal. If we heard anyone in their compartments, we planned to knock and see if there were any special meal requests," she finished, rubbing her nose.

Plausible. Much better than anything Fina could come up with in the moment, which was nothing.

Ridgewell folded his arms, still smirking. "Well, yes, now you mention it, I'd like spotted dick for dessert. Been craving that for a while. What do you say, Mother and Dot?" He looked over his shoulder at his family. They nodded.

"Right you are. Spotted dick," said Ruby.

As soon as they entered the lounge, Ada waved them over to her seat near a corner window. "Come here, *Mäuschen*," she said. "I have something to discuss with you."

"What is it Oma Ada?" asked Ruby as she sat down next to her.

"*Tja*, I do not like it, I do not like it at all," she said as she wound yarn around one hand.

"Yes?" asked Fina.

"Father Schweinsteiger. There is something very suspicious about him."

Fina's stomach lurched. The priest was peculiar. And yet she couldn't suppress a flutter of anxiety about trusting Ada Hartman, who had grown up in one of the most pro-Nazi towns in Germany.

Ada leaned over and whispered, "I do not believe he is Swiss. I think he is German. The question is, why would he lie about it?"

"Is he lying about it? Does he deny it?" asked Ruby.

"When I ask him about it directly, he denies it. I can tell by the accent. I don't understand why he needs to lie about it. It would be perfectly normal for him to be from Germany. And he must know that I know!"

"Hmmm … yes, that is true. He must know that you know, so why deny it? Do you think he's under some strain so he's not thinking clearly?"

"Well, that's certainly plain from his card-playing," said Ada with a wry smile. "He is a compulsive one."

"Ah! There you are, Frau Hartman!" came a voice from behind them. Father Felix Schweinsteiger stood next to them. How long had he been in the lounge? Fina could have sworn he wasn't there just a moment ago.

"Are you ready for another round of cards? I feel quite refreshed. This time I will win."

"Of course you will, *Vater*," said Ada with a ghost of a smile. As she rose, she set her knitting bag on the chair as if to save her seat. As the oldest person on the train, she was entitled to whichever seat she chose.

As Ada wobbled toward the card table, Father Felix turned back toward Ruby and Fina. He held up his hand to his mouth and said in a conspiratorial whisper, "Frau Hartman isn't as harmless as she looks."

Fina caught her breath. Had he, too, made the connection with Braunschweig? Surely not everyone from Braunschweig sympathised with the National Socialists.

"She's a ruthless one for cards," added Felix.

Fina smiled in relief, and was joined by Ruby. Frau Hartman might be particularly skilled at cards, but there was also a chance that Felix was particularly unskilled.

"And I'll tell you one more thing. That pair – the author of filth and her *secretary*," he said, a great deal of emphasis on the word 'secretary'. "They're very suspicious. You should watch yourself around them."

"You believe them to be dangerous?" asked Ruby with an air of disbelief.

He nodded. "*Ja*. I do not trust those who write blasphemous material for a living."

A GRUMBLING MAURICE led the trio into the galley. Laurent consented to their assistance in the kitchen as long as Maurice could watch them closely – in case they tried to tamper with the food.

As one might have expected, the galley was large enough for a line of people as thin as wafers. Though short, Pixley was a bit broader than Maurice. Even though Pixley was the best chef among the trio, he said he'd pop back to the lounge car to have a word with Etienne – or maybe even a little interview.

Maurice continued to mumble underneath his breath in French. Fina caught several unkind words about women. She and Ruby washed their hands and stood at attention like army cadets ready for inspection.

Maurice softened a bit at their display. Fina detected

the slightest curve of the mouth underneath that stubble.

He pointed to a bowl of vegetables near the basin and mimed a cutting action. They went to work and soon the galley was redolent with the smells of Maurice's cooking. Fina's spirits lifted a little as she snatched a carrot here and a slice of bread there.

"How long have you been working on *Train Blanc*?" asked Ruby in a casual voice.

"Five years," was the staccato answer.

"Do you enjoy it?" asked Fina.

"Yes. People like to 'ave good food on a train. It is an event."

"Anything you don't like about your work?" asked Ruby.

He waved a spoon around the room. Ruby and Fina dodged the flying drops of red sauce. "This space! Being an artist here, it is impossible. And there are too many foreigners on this train," he growled.

Ruby and Fina shot knowing glances at one another.

Slam. His cleaver came down on the cutting board. Then he wiped his bloody hands on his white apron.

"Oh, ah. Well. Are there more foreigners than usual?" asked Ruby.

"I do not like all these meal requests! Every nationality, they want to eat the cuisine of their own country. Swiss, German, Russian, Italian, Egyptian, Spanish,

Portuguese ... and English! That is the worst. It is not a cuisine. It is a farce!"

Fina and Ruby were saved from having to respond – or tell Maurice about Ridgewell's request for spotted dick – when Julien poked his head into the galley. "The list is complete. Please join us in the dining car when the lunch is ready and we will pass it along."

20

"Mr Durand?"

Pixley slid into the rounded armchair next to Etienne. "I say, this isn't the best time to talk about world politics, but it might help distract us both from our predicament. What do you say – how about an interview?"

Etienne's eyes flickered. "Why?" he said, straightening up in his chair. He threw down the newspaper he must have read at least five times by now. "I am usually not so crass, but exhaustion tends to strip away all social niceties. What's in it for me, as our American friends might say?"

Pixley licked his lips. "Since you're being direct, I'll follow suit. At some point – hopefully in the near future – we'll all disembark from this train. When we do, I will be the one to write the story for newspapers clamouring for an inside scoop. This is your opportunity to tell me about the purpose of those Paris negotiations, rather than having me – or other journalists – simply speculate."

A wry smile spread across Etienne's handsome face. "You're certainly persuasive, Mr Hayford. I'll do as you ask, on one condition."

"Yes?"

"That if I say something I want to retract, you will honour the retraction and not just pretend to do so."

Pixley held up his hand. "I shall do so. On my honour."

"Hmph. For whatever that's worth, coming from a journalist," chuckled Etienne. "Go on, what do you want to know?"

"What, exactly, do these negotiations concern?"

Etienne folded his hands in his lap and stared with fascination at the blue flower patterns on the sofa opposite. "France is concerned about recent aggressive moves by Germany, as I'm sure you're well aware."

"My sources tell me the development of a Nazi *Reichswehr* military force has the British Foreign Office very concerned."

"Yes, these are troubling times," said Etienne as he rubbed his forehead.

"What about aggressive moves of Italy in Ethiopia, which you and the British allowed to happen? It wasn't until I visited Italy that I realised how serious things had become. First, the British and the French allow Italy to build up their military on the border of Ethiopia. Then, after Mussolini used what was probably a made-up incident as an excuse to invade Ethiopia, the British condemn the action. Seems as though Mussolini has called the British government's bluff on that point, since the invasion is well underway without any sign of a challenge – at least by any European powers."

Etienne worked his jaw. "I thought you were a journalist, Mr Hayford. Don't you want a story? It's no secret that I have spoken with representatives of the Italian state. In fact, we have made some headway on many issues. But remember, I do not set policies – I carry out the negotiations."

Pixley bit off an easy retort. "Forgive me, I'm a little punchy given the events of the past twenty-four hours. Please do go on."

Julian materialised. "I'm sorry, *monsieurs*, but may I offer you coffee or tea?" he asked, presenting trays with both hot liquids.

"Coffee – no, better make that tea," said Pixley with a shudder, remembering Neeya.

"Coffee, please," said Etienne, apparently not remembering or not caring about the significance of coffee. "To return to the issue at hand," he said, blowing on his coffee and grimacing at the first sip. "The best course of action, at least according to the current French government, is to ally itself with Soviet power against the Germans. There is a general sentiment they are the only ones able to keep Germany in check."

"Will you be negotiating with Stalin himself?" asked Pixley as he doctored his cup of tea with ample milk and sugar.

Etienne's forehead wrinkled in horror. "No, no, of course not. He will send representatives to Paris," he said, waving his hands about. "I am confident we can come to an agreement – if I ever arrive in Paris."

"What are the consequences of a late arrival into Paris?"

Etienne flew out of his chair and began to pace. "Disastrous. It's not that I am so important as myself – as in my personality, Etienne – but I am the only one who has established relationships with the Soviet negotiators. My deputy, Pierre Maurin, has excellent Russian and a good grasp of recent political history, but *il n'a pas de cran* – in your language, he lacks the guts. Plus, the Soviets have never taken to him. Stalin is notoriously suspicious, and if Maurin steps in to take my place, Stalin will undoubtedly interpret it as a conspiracy by the British or the Germans – or whomever he happens to mistrust when he eats his breakfast in the morning."

"Who else has interests in these talks? Anyone besides the British and the Germans?"

"Well, there are several political groups on the left and right. Some attached to various national struggles and some not. They would be interested in swaying these talks in one direction or another. Or would wish to halt them altogether."

Pixley peered at Etienne as he sipped his milky tea. He set aside his notebook and pen. "Now, Mr Durand. Do you want to tell me what you're really doing on this train?"

21

"Excuse me, gentlemen," said Laurent, interrupting a staring match between Etienne and Pixley. "We must move to the dining room to discuss something of great importance."

Pixley, apparently satisfied to let his provocative question linger in the air, jumped up and toddled after Laurent into the dining car.

Ruby patted the seat next to her as Pixley and Laurent entered. A reluctant and wary-eyed Etienne followed.

"What did you find out?" hissed Fina from across the table.

Pixley waved at Fina and then made a motion of locking his lips.

Laurent stood in the middle of the dining room as Julien and Maurice served lunch to the passengers.

"May I have your attention? We have completed the search of everyone's compartments, as well as their persons, with the able assistance of Mrs Hartman," he said, bowing his head in Ada's direction. "Our gentleman thief has directed us to share this list with all the passengers. He hopes it might spark a hidden memory about the murders. After we have finished this task, Mr Hayford will deliver the list to the thief. He has assured us that after he has received the list, he will decide whether the train can continue to its destination." He paused. "Rather than read this lengthy list aloud, I will let each of you read it to yourselves while you eat lunch." He wrinkled his nose. "Even though I disapprove of any distraction such as reading while one is eating."

Maurice looked up and mumbled approval at this last statement.

The trio sat alone at their lunch table. Fina wondered if their lack of company was due to Pixley's enquiring mind – as well as his association with the 'gentleman thief'. At least they could continue their ruminations in private. They had agreed Fina would take notes about any unusual exclamations or reactions to the list as passengers had their turn at reading it.

After some moments of silence, broken only by the *clink* of cutlery, Etienne Durand looked up and directed a stony stare at Ridgewell. "Mr Synge, I must protest most strongly," said Etienne. "You are indeed a talented artist, but I did not authorise any portraiture of myself and neither, I suspect, did the others." He glanced around the room for support.

Father Schweinsteiger pointed a fork at Ridgewell. "Yes, I demand you tear them up. Immediately."

Other guests clamoured against the unauthorised portraits. Defeated, Ridgewell stamped out of the dining car.

"Why does Raoul have a Spanish *and* a French passport?" asked Dot, displaying her analytical mind once again.

"Because I was born on the border between the two countries," said Raoul in a huff.

Dot shrugged.

"Speaking of passports," said Eustace, "why does our dear Mrs Hartman have German, Swiss, Italian and French passports?"

"I enjoy travelling and living in different locations, Herr Wistow," she said, not looking up from her knitting. She seemed completely unfazed by the question.

"Why does the Synge family have tickets for a cruise from Cairo?" asked Raoul, grinning mischievously.

"Is it a crime to take a cruise?" asked Dot.

Madeline put a hand on her daughter's arm. "It's true. We were in Egypt. But the political situation there, has, well, hotted up, shall we say? We decided to return home at a leisurely pace."

"What were you doing in Egypt?" asked Ruby.

"We were attached to the embassy there. The British embassy, of course. My husband died of a heart attack a year ago. We thought we'd stay on but, as I say, the situation became untenable."

"Was your maiden name Hinton?" asked Ruby.

"Yes," said Madeline as she played with the edge of one sleeve of her frock. "Ridgewell decided to take my maiden name as his last name. That's why he has the two passports with him in case there are any difficulties at the border."

"But why did Ridgewell change his name?" asked Ruby.

"If you must know, he didn't get on well with our father," said Dot. "As soon as Daddy died, my brother changed his last name."

Fina surveyed the room. The other passengers looked as unconvinced as she was.

Dot lashed out. "Well, since we're clearing the air," she said, peering sourly around the room, "Mrs Hartman and Father Schweinsteiger both seem to have quite impressive reserves of European currency stashed away in their rooms, whereas some of us – Raoul, for instance – have almost nothing. How come the two of you can afford to travel in such luxury?"

Passengers let out squeaks, gulps, and gasps. Raoul looked abashed.

Still focusing intently on her hideous knitting, Ada

replied, "My husband left me a great deal of money. I enjoy using it to travel, as I already mentioned."

Father Schweinsteiger, on the other hand, rubbed his neck with his finger, underneath his collar. "I come from a wealthy family in Switzerland. My father wanted me to join the family business but I decided instead to become a man of the cloth."

A likely story. As minor recriminations continued, Fina focused on the list which had been handed to her. With Ruby's guidance, she noted the items of possible importance in her notebook:

DOROTHY SYNGE — Cruise tickets (for family) from Cairo to Brindisi. November 1, 1935.

Madeline Synge — Sophia Salazar's books.

Ridgewell Synge — Sketches. Two British passports. One under the name Hinton.

Sophia Salazar — Collected poems of Fernando Pessoa.

Raoul Lapointe — Photograph of young woman. Rifle slung over shoulder. Back of the photo reads "Inez, Tarragona, 1934."

James Matua — Receipt for pistol.

Eustace Wistow — Copy of The Decline and Fall of the British Empire. *Letters to friends in Leeward islands. Return ticket stubs from Cairo to Rome flight for a week in October.*

Ada Hartman — Multiple passports: German, Swiss, Ital-

ian, and French. Decks of cards, knitting supplies. Great deal of banknotes in various currencies.

Neeya Arafa – Flyer in notebook from nationalist groups. Nothing written in journal about nationalist support.

Felix Schweinsteiger – German and Swiss passport. Multiple volumes of Tolstoy, Chekov, and Dostoevsky in Russian.

Etienne Durand – Various diplomatic documents about Italian negotiations over Ethiopia. Russian newspaper clippings. Appointment book.

"Mr Wistow, why did you travel to Cairo?" asked Fina.

"Wanted to tour the Valley of the Kings and all that," he said, tapping his cigarette on an ashtray. No ash fell from the cigarette.

Ridgewell returned, still in a fury. He held his sketchbook in one hand and Ricki, the cat, in the other. "I found the kitten wandering the corridor, so I thought he ought to join us in here," he said, handing the cat to Raoul.

"Ricki! I told you to stay in the cabin," said Raoul, affecting a stern look. He was so taken up with cooing over the kitten and jingling its collar that he never noticed Ridgewell's glare. Now there, thought Fina, is a man who loves his cat – perhaps a little too much.

Even though Ridgewell was decidedly taciturn – at least around his sister – he certainly had a flair for the dramatic. He tore out his sketches of individual passengers and shredded them in half. As each drawing required this elaborate gesture, the faces of passengers displayed great embarrassment. Flipping through the rest of the sketchbook, he said, "Where are the other drawings? Who tore them out?" He peered around the room. "Well?" he said, putting his hands on his hips.

Dot interrupted the theatre. "Are you sure you didn't tear them out yourself?"

"Of course not. Someone has been snooping in my compartment."

Silence.

Madeline intervened. "What about the train crew?"

Maurice, who had been sitting sulking in a corner, crept toward Madeline with murderous intent in his eyes. Julien sprang lightly from his seat and blocked the way.

Laurent nodded and smiled at Julien. "We thought you might be interested in that, so we each searched one another's cabins," he said, lighting a cigarette and producing the list. Ruby's hand shot up immediately so he offered it to her. Ruby read the list aloud:

"Laurent Belrose – Betting slips from Monte Carlo.

Maurice Gaudin – A copy of *La Cuisine en Dix Minutes, ou L'Adaptation au Rhythme Moderne*, many boxes of toothpicks and letters from 'Maria'.

Julien Paquet – Compagnie Internationale des Wagons Lits – a manual. *The Savoury Cocktail Book*."

"SEEMS IN ORDER, WHAT?" said Eustace, swirling his brandy snifter.

"If everyone has read the list, it's time for Mr Hayford to deliver it to our gentleman thief," said Laurent.

"Tell him we have urgent appointments, Mr Hayford," said Etienne. "Which may be a matter of life and death."

"Good luck, Pixley," whispered Ruby and Fina.

22

Fresh glass of scotch in hand, Pixley pocketed the list and strode off toward the front of the train.

He knocked on the train carriage door nearest the engine. Ian popped up and peered through the glass. He opened the window and waved in Pixley.

"Where's the engine driver?" asked Pixley.

"He's napping. Come, tell me what you've found," Ian said. Pixley produced the list. He handed over the glass of scotch. Ian sipped a minute amount and said, "Ah, that's precisely what I needed. Thanks, old man."

They sat together on a wooden bench, the engine's coal fire blazing away beside them. Ian peered at the list, his eyebrows wiggling as he concentrated, while Pixley twirled his spectacles meditatively. Pixley smiled at how Ian's close-cropped hair barely hid a tiny thinning patch on his head, even though he was only in his mid-twenties. Ian's only outward flaw in an otherwise strikingly handsome figure.

"You realise you can't keep this up much longer," said Pixley.

"Shhh ... I haven't finished yet," said Ian, taking another sip of scotch. Finally, he folded up the list and pocketed it. "Intriguing points."

"Care to share what they might be?" Pixley asked, wiping his brow. The room was stifling.

Ian shook his head and slapped Pixley on the back. "Sorry, Pix, it's nothing definite."

Pixley burst out, "First you tell me to take this train. Then you put me in the awkward position of having to pull a gun on the train conductor so I could make contact with you! I have to lie to Ruby and Fina. Then everyone on the train thinks I'm collaborating with you – which I am, at obviously great personal risk. Now you won't even let me in on what you're thinking?" Both of Pixley's legs jiggled furiously, causing his spectacles to wobble.

In a calm voice, Ian said, "I know you're upset. And you're completely justified. If there were another way to do this, I would do it. And I'm not lying when I say there's nothing definite. There are a few points of interest which mean nothing right now – I need to ruminate."

Pixley's legs came to a slow halt. He sighed. A tremendously loud sigh.

"How is Ruby?" asked Ian, eyes shining.

"She's furious with you, and I can't say as I blame her," said Pixley. "But I do have to say she was a touch overwrought – for Ruby, anyway."

Ian grinned. "Well, at least I can hold on to that," he said, pausing. "Now, here's what we need to do. I need you to escort Governor Wistow here. I must have a conversation with him. You're welcome to stay and listen, as long as you don't turn on that reporter-brain of yours. After that, I must talk to Etienne Durand. Then I will explain myself to everyone, and we will proceed to Lausanne. I doubt this train will travel all the way to Paris after what has happened."

Pixley shook his head. "I haven't any idea how we'll escape this alive – or at the very least, without going to prison for a long time."

Ian winked. "I always have something up my sleeve, Pix."

⁓

"MR WISTOW, PLEASE HAVE A SEAT," said Ian, pulling down his scarf from his face. He motioned as if the train carriage were a grand palace.

Eustace Wistow sat opposite Ian on another wooden bench.

"Brandy?" offered Pixley, holding a decanter he had brought with him from the lounge.

The governor grunted his affirmation. "Now, what the devil are you doing, man?" he asked Pixley irritably. "Do you want to get us all killed with this murderous maniac on the loose? It's easy for you, you're separated from the rest of us. And –" he turned to Ian "– what are *you* doing playing at being a train robber? Watched one too many films?" Eustace's moustache shook.

"I am well aware of the situation, which is why I want to speed this process up as much as possible. And that's why I've asked you here," said Ian.

"Well, go on, man, out with it."

"You were governor of the Leeward islands from 1920 to 1933, correct?"

"Yes, what of it?"

"And are you familiar with the Haitian Revolution?"

"Of course."

"And you must be aware of one of your earlier colonial predecessors: Governor of Barbados, Lord Seaforth?"

"Afraid not. What's this to do with anything? Have you taken leave of your senses, son?"

Ian walked to one end of the car and quickly spun before he reached the door. He repeated this exercise up and down the length of the train car, hands clasped behind his back.

"Lord Seaforth was a rare colonial governor of the 1800s, regardless of his motives. Did you know he made it a capital offence for a white person to kill an enslaved person?"

"That may be, but how is it relevant now? Besides, I'm no longer governor."

"But you have friends in high places, in addition to being in the House of Lords. I also understand the current governor is your nephew. He must trust you and take your advice."

Eustace ran his hands through his thinning hair. "Well, yes. But the boy doesn't take my advice half of the time I give it to him. Arrogance of youth and all that rot."

"Nevertheless, you do have influence," said Ian, reaching the end of the carriage. He spun around, eyes glowing. "And I suppose you must know about the so-called labour disturbances of the past two years, not only in the Leeward Islands but also around the Caribbean?"

"Of course, of course. 'Disturbances' is the right word for it. Stops up oil and sugar production. Not good for the British economy."

Ian smiled. "I'm sure that's how you view it. But you see, from the perspective of those who are creating these so-called disturbances, the situation is different. I suppose you can admit that."

Eustace hesitated. "Well ... yes, I suppose they might have a different perspective. But it still doesn't change the fact it hurts Britain."

"I'm not here to discuss the merits of colonialism, Mr Wistow. I'm here to direct you on behalf of those who created those disturbances."

"Still don't understand what I can do, son."

Ian lost his temper momentarily. "I'm not your son. Let's stop this affable old-boy-colonel posture, shall we?"

Eustace said nothing. But then grunted in apparent approval.

"Here's what you're going to do—" Ian began.

Eustace rose to his feet. "I'll thank you to stop this nonsense, young man! I've half a mind to bring this talk to a close this very minute. Why should I agree to anything you say?" He stood and turned, as if to leave the carriage.

"I'll tell you why," replied Ian. *"Eulalie."*

Eustace whirled round. He stared at Ian, his moustache drooping, along with his shoulders. "Did you say Eulalie?"

"Yes."

"Oh."

"Yes, oh," said Ian. "I see I've convinced you," he added with a satisfied smile. "And don't forget, I said that in the presence of a journalist."

Eustace sputtered, "But, but, you can't have told him! I won't do anything now. How may I be certain you won't use it anyway, no matter what I say?"

"You don't, but you have little choice in the matter. Trust me, I have not told Mr Hayford, and will only tell him if you do not hold up your end of the bargain."

"How can I trust you?" asked Eustace.

"Well, consider this for a moment. I could have exposed you in front of all the passengers, and still tried to ask you to do something. Instead, I kept it quiet, and will also keep your reputation intact – if you follow my instructions carefully."

Eustace said nothing but waved his hands in resignation.

"I'll take that as an affirmative gesture," said Ian. "Now, you will instruct your nephew, the current governor, to have a trial – which is not rigged – for those plantation owners. The trial will concern those involved in the massacre which occurred last month after a labour strike. I'm sure it's a familiar story to you – it was in all of the newspapers. I'll jog your memory. After plantation owners continued to slash cane-worker wages, the workers went on strike in St Kitts. They marched to one of the more egregious plantations, where the owner informed them they were trespassing. A series of skirmishes ensued over the next few days, culminating in a protest at the same estate. One of the owners hit the workers with pellet guns, causing the crowd to become increasingly agitated. Government forces arrived with live ammunition and a warship was called in from Bermuda. The government read the Riot Act and the crowd threw stones in response. Chaos ensued and shots were fired – obviously by the government since they were the ones with the weapons. Three people were killed and eight wounded. And the cane fields burned."

Eustace nodded. "Yes, I did know generally what happened, but I didn't know those details."

"You are to direct your nephew to halt all military protection of the plantation owners' interests. If there is a strike, the government will not intervene – and if it is necessary, no violence will be inflicted on the strikers, nor will their leaders be targeted for jail time. In other words, the government will stop propping up the plantation economy."

Eustace stammered, "That's a tall order, son – I mean, sir. What if my nephew refuses?"

"That's your problem, not mine. I'm sure someone as clever as yourself can figure out ways, especially since you made a mint as governor."

Ian nodded to Pixley. "That's all. You may go now, Mr Wistow. Mr Hayford will arrange for me to talk to Mr Durand next, and then we'll be on our way to Lausanne."

"What am I to tell the others?"

"Whatever you like, as long as it's not the truth."

Eustace and Pixley padded toward the door.

"One moment, Mr Wistow," said Ian, holding up a hand. "If you breathe a word about this to the police in any investigation of this little train incident, I will tell all the world about Eulalie. Is that clear?"

Eustace's shoulders slumped, but he nodded. Pixley turned and winked at Ian as they returned to the dining carriage.

23

———

Fina slapped the ace of diamonds on the table. "I wonder what in the world Ian could be discussing with Eustace. Does it have something to do with the labour uprisings in the Caribbean?"

Ruby peered through the window. Hail pelted the windows and ceiling, creating a simultaneously disturbing and cosy effect. "I expect that must be what it's about. I'm sure he's being very persuasive," she said with a twisty smile.

Pixley entered with a ghost-like Eustace. He wobbled and weaved like a roly-poly toy. Pixley offered him another drink and settled him into a chair as if he were tucking in a child to bed for the night. The few other passengers who remained in the lounge looked over, ready to pounce. But then apparently thought better of it.

Pixley trundled over to join them, but not before absently popping a chocolate into his mouth. He must be beyond caring if it were poisoned. Pulling up a chair backwards, he leaned his head on the frame. Ruby rubbed his hand. "Thank you. You must be exhausted. We know you cannot tell us anything, but we'll continue our conversation and hopefully you'll reveal something with your ever-expressive facial gestures," she chuckled.

"Go on. I can pass any test," he said with a smile and then a desperate sigh.

"We were chatting about our friend the governor," said Fina, eyeing the box of chocolates Pixley had opened. It wasn't worth the risk, even for chocolate. "We were saying we expect this all has something to do with the labour disturbances in the Caribbean."

Pixley's face remained impassive. Then his head bobbed upward. "Fina, I've never understood why you're involved in these campaigns – I understood your dislike of Gasthorpe at Oxford because of his anti-Irish politics, but I don't understand the relationship to the Caribbean."

Fina cleared her throat. "Besides the fact we share a common threat – which is the British Empire – the Irish have a special history in the Caribbean."

Pixley adjusted his spectacles and peered at Fina, apparently welcoming the distraction. "Go on. I'm completely ignorant."

"In the 1600s, the British sent Irish political prisoners and religious people to St Kitts. Montserrat was seventy per cent Irish slaves at one time – that's why it's called the 'Emerald Isle' in the Caribbean. I have a few distant relatives who live there."

"But surely you're not trying to compare the two forms of slavery," said Pixley.

"No, no, I wouldn't do that. It's just that there is a common history in resisting British rule. Rather than trying to resist the British alone, it makes sense for us to join together."

"Feens is a visionary," said Ruby.

"That's the nicest compliment you've ever paid, me, Ruby, but you're the one who is the visionary. I follow the lead – quite happily," smiled Fina.

"If this mutual appreciation society meeting is over," said Pixley, "I must get on. I sent Laurent to retrieve Etienne from his compartment but he hasn't returned yet. I'd better find out what's keeping him."

Pixley toddled off toward the sleeping cars.

Fina banged the table. "Why won't Pixley tell us what's going on? It's making me as bad-tempered as a bag of weasels."

"Believe me, I'm as peeved as you are, Feens," said Ruby, smoothing her hair. "But there has to be a reason he's keeping it from us."

A sudden noise made them both jump. "Did you hear that?" asked Fina.

"Sounded like shouting. We'd better find Pixley. And fast."

"WOULD you help me with this, Mr Hayford?" asked Laurent as Pixley approached.

"What's the matter?"

"I've knocked on the door of Mr Durand several times. Then I tried to unlock it. I turned the key, but the door, it seems to be jammed."

The pair pushed and pulled. No luck.

By now, the ruckus had attracted the attention of other passengers in the carriage. Ricki was perched on Raoul's shoulder. He mewed plaintively at the situation.

"We need *un levier*," said Laurent. "The lever. But whatever it is must be small and thin."

"Like metal knitting needles?" offered Raoul.

"Bingo!" said Pixley.

"Did someone say something about knitting?" asked Ada. She rushed down the hallway, flush with the colour of someone who had won yet another game of cards against Father Schweinsteiger.

"Yes, Mrs Hartman. May we borrow your knitting needles? It's an emergency," said Laurent.

Ada disappeared into her compartment. Minutes passed. Sophia bent her head around the door of Ada's cabin. "Something amiss, Mrs Hartman?"

"*Quatsch!*" came the reply. "They've disappeared. My knitting needles."

"Let me help you," said Sophia. "Perhaps they rolled underneath the sofa."

Ada and Sophia emerged from the cabin empty-handed.

Ada held up one finger. "Ach, I left my knitting bag in the lounge. Give me just a moment to retrieve it," she said, without waiting for anyone's approval to do so.

"Mrs Hartman, where are you going?" asked Fina as she and Ruby approached her in the hallway.

"My knitting needles – or my knitting bag. I believe I left them in the lounge. Do you remember?"

"I do remember you left your bag on the chair in the lounge," said Ruby.

"*Danke.* I will find it." Ada waved at them as she moved toward the front of the train.

"Wonder why she needs them so urgently," said Fina.

Soon, they arrived at Etienne's compartment to find Laurent and Pixley trying to open the door.

Ruby opened her clutch, removed a nail file, and gave it to Laurent. "This could dislodge whatever is jammed in the doorframe," she said.

Laurent wiggled the nail file around the hinges, dislodging several handkerchiefs which someone had stuffed into the doorframe.

The nail file dropped to the floor.

Laurent pulled the door open, glanced in, then rapidly backed away from the cabin, quivering from head to toe.

24

"Please, please, do not look," said Laurent, even as Pixley stepped into the compartment.

His request had the unfortunate effect of driving everyone closer to the cabin.

Pixley stepped out of the cabin and blocked the entry with his solid frame. "Mr Belrose is correct. No one needs to see that."

Ruby stood close to Pixley. He leaned over and whispered, "Not even you, Ruby. I'll tell you what you need to know."

Laurent looked gratefully at Pixley as he stood in the doorway. "I suggest we all reconvene in the lounge. We need to track where everyone was in the last hour."

Heads bent in apparent resignation, the passengers filed past the closed door to Etienne's compartment.

Dot whispered to her mother, "Must be the German

woman and her knitting needles. I knew that sweet grandmother persona was all an act."

"But anyone could have taken those knitting needles. In any case, wouldn't it be difficult for her to overpower Etienne? He was relatively petite, but still..." Madeline trailed off.

Raoul said, "I sensed this train was cursed from the start. My tarot readings told me so. But no, you insisted on this day and this train, Sophia," he said, nearly spitting at his employer.

Sophia looked unperturbed by his accusation. "If the journey had been smooth, you probably would have said your tarot cards said it would be so."

"Would not!" he said.

Ricki hissed from Raoul's shoulder.

"Please! Mr Lapointe and Miss Salazar," said Laurent in an exasperated voice. "We must go to the lounge. Now."

The pair slunk off toward the lounge, followed by Laurent and then Ruby.

Ow. Fina's shin hit one of the folding seats, which flopped open in the corridor. As she stood there rubbing her leg, a scraping noise came from behind her. Turning, she spied Julien unlocking Etienne's cabin.

Selkies and kelpies! The pain clouded her mind so she stood there, not knowing what to do next. She certainly didn't want to view Etienne's body, but that was what would happen if she confronted Julien.

As the pain subsided, she decided it was not only better for her eyes, but for her safety, to not be alone with him. She didn't suspect Julien of being the murderer for one moment, but her instincts told her it was better to tell Ruby. Or to confront Julien in the relative safety provided by a crowd of passengers.

She limped to the lounge. Ruby stood in the doorway, peering back into the darkness of the corridor. "There you are! I had a heart-stopping moment of worry. Are you injured?"

"Only temporarily. Hit my shin on something."

Ruby piloted Fina to a nearby chair. She sat down next to her. Ruby said, "Laurent was beginning to review the whereabouts of everyone in the last hour."

"How are we going to do that? Everyone is constantly coming and going on this train – despite the fact there are so few cars!"

"I believe he's about to explain."

Laurent had given up the pretence of the conductor's cap a few hours earlier so this time he simply ran his hands through his hair as he prepared to speak. "First, let me thank you all for remaining calm during these trying circumstances. I am surprised and grateful that none of you have – what is the English expression? Gone—"

"Round the bend?" said Madeline.

"Crackers?" supplied her daughter.

Laurent grimaced at the idioms but bowed his head

in gratitude. "Someone killed Mr Durand within the last hour," he said, glancing at his watch. "That is when I noticed him retire to his cabin. He said he was going to take a nap."

Father Schweinsteiger said, "I can confirm it's true. I watched him leave the lounge."

"Now, as you're all aware, there are two sleeping cars. Mr Durand's compartment is located in the carriage closest to the lounge. Julien," he said, waving his hand to the seat usually occupied by the attendant, "who must be assisting Maurice in the galley..."

Assisting, my foot. Did Laurent know why Julien was missing? Fina couldn't tell from his expression.

"Julien sat in the rear sleeping carriage at the attendant's fold-out seat in the corridor. He could watch everyone coming and going in that cabin. I, myself, sat in the lounge – waiting for news from Mr Hayford."

"So you're saying that between the two of you, we can determine who had the opportunity to kill Mr Durand," said Ruby. "And I assume he was killed with Mrs Hartman's knitting needles, correct?"

Ada covered her face with her hands. *"Mein Gott,"* she whispered.

Sophia and Raoul sat nearest Fina. Their faces had taken on an earthy, mouldy colour. Fina took in deep breaths as she tried not to picture the scene.

"Precisely, Miss Dove," said Laurent. Julien slipped

into the lounge like a cat, padding over and curling up in his usual chair.

"I'll begin with what I observed in the lounge," continued Laurent. "Miss Dove and Miss Aubrey-Havelock sat at one table, playing cards. Later, Monsieur Hayford entered with Governor Wistow, from the front of the train."

"Did any of them leave during that time?" asked Dot.

"Miss Dove did. Would you care to explain, Mademoiselle?" asked Laurent.

Ruby rose and stood as if she were about to provide court testimony. "Yes, I went to our cabin to retrieve a favourite pack of playing cards, and to use the lavatory."

Julien nodded. "I watched Mademoiselle Dove do as she said," he replied.

"But she could have pilfered the knitting needles from Mrs Hartman's cabin and then snuck into Etienne's cabin – on her way to her compartment or on the return journey," said Dot.

Laurent nodded, "Yes, I did not examine my watch during that time, so we do not know how long it took her. Though we can ask her card-playing partner," he said, turning to Fina.

"Ruby was absent for about the amount of time you'd expect to complete those two tasks," she replied.

"If that's true, Miss Aubrey-Havelock," sneered Dot, "why is your face brick-red, as if you're concealing something?"

Blast the woman. "I have little control over what shade of colour my face turns. If anyone accuses me of something or questions my honesty, my face will usually turn red. Regardless of the situation."

"I used to have the same problem, *Schatz*," said Mrs Hartman, smiling empathetically at Fina.

"Thank you, Mrs Hartman," said Fina, turning up her nose at Dot. "In any case, if Ruby were a practised hand at being a murderer, I suppose she might have committed the crime. But that seems rather unlikely, doesn't it?"

"Thank you, Miss Aubrey-Havelock. Now, Father Schweinsteiger and Mrs Hartman were the other passengers in the lounge during that time. The Father left the cabin briefly, correct?" Laurent turned toward the priest.

He nodded. "*Ja*, I had a call of the wild."

"Ah, I believe you mean a call of nature, old boy," said Eustace. Eustace had not moved since his interview with Ian. He appeared to be rooted to his chair.

"*Ja,* I did that. It was only for a few minutes," he replied. Ada nodded her assent.

"But he still might have done it," offered Raoul.

"Yes, but he would have had to have been very quick."

Julien said, "As for Monsieur Lapointe, he could have committed the crime as well. He left his compartment during that time."

"Yes," replied Raoul, stiffening. "I needed to fetch a saucer of milk from Maurice to feed Ricki."

"*Bien,*" said Laurent. "That leaves the Synges. Neither I nor Julien saw them. They are the ones with the greatest opportunity. This is because their cabins are located in the same sleeping carriage as Monsieur Durand's and Madame Hartman's compartments."

"I protest!" yelped Dot, standing and folding her arms.

Her mother patted her on the back. "Sit down, dear. Mr Belrose is just reviewing the possibilities."

"He's trying to implicate us, Mother. He's had something against us from the beginning. See his shifty eyes!"

In what was clearly an involuntary gesture, Laurent's hand flew up to his eyes. "No, no, Miss Synge. As your mother said, I try to understand how this happened," he said, then changed tack. "Since you were in the cabin, did any of you hear anything?"

Dot sat back down but still left her arms crossed. "No, I was asleep the entire time. I stuff cotton wool in my ears because of Mother's snoring."

Fina wondered if Madeline ever considered what she had done as a mother to deserve this child.

Madeline replied, "When I sleep, I sleep very heavily – even if it's only for a short time. I heard nothing."

All eyes slid toward Ridgewell. "Oh – er – I nodded off between sketches," he said, furrowing his brow. "But

I do remember drifting off and then being shaken into consciousness by shuffling and scraping noises."

"No cries or groans?" asked Laurent.

"No. Just the shuffling. As if someone were moving something heavy around in their compartment."

Everyone shuddered.

"This means the only people who can be eliminated as suspects are Miss Salazar, Miss Aubrey-Havelock, Mr Hayford, and Mrs Hartman."

"Has anyone seen Pixley?" asked Ruby. "He was sitting here a moment ago but seems to have vanished."

A voice came from the doorway, with a faint trace of a Bahamian accent: "We're here."

25

———

Everyone's necks whipped round to the front of the train.

There, standing in the doorway, was Pixley, and next to him stood Ian. Dapper and dashing as ever, Ian wore a blue silk ascot, a tailored grey suit, and a sharp fedora. He looked like he had walked off the stage on the opening night of one of his glitzy West End productions, as he'd done so often, rather than from the engine of a train.

"It's him! The thief!" screamed Dot. She cowered in her chair.

Ridgewell murmured unkind racial epithets under his breath. Fina glared at him. Mrs Synge also glared at her son.

Eustace's face turned a pale brown pasty colour. Almost like a croissant.

Sophia blew smoke rings, while Raoul removed what appeared to be imaginary lint from his suit.

Father Schweinsteiger made the sign of the cross.

In the silence, all Fina heard was the puncture noises made by Ada Hartman's needlepoint. A wise choice after what had happened with her knitting needles.

Pixley pointed at Ian and took a little bow, as if introducing royalty. "May I present Mr Rampton."

Brilliant. Better to use a pseudonym, just in case. Come to that, though, how did she know 'Ian Clavering' was his real name in the first place? Maybe that was a cover as well. He might be named Antonio Darling for all she knew.

Several passengers continued to cower in their seats. Others stared. Only Mrs Hartman appeared unfazed.

Ruby's body was as stiff as a fishing rod.

Ian removed his hat and held it over his heart. He gave a little bow. "Dear passengers, I do regret the extreme inconvenience. I was put in this position under complex circumstances. The powers-that-be forced my hand. Now that someone has committed these tragic murders – completely unconnected to our little stop here in the beautiful Alps," he said, gesturing toward the window with his hat, "I thought it best I come forward so we can all find out the identity of the criminal."

"I'll tell you who the criminal is," muttered Raoul under his breath.

Ian either didn't hear this remark or simply ignored it. "I understand from Mr Hayford here that a Miss Ruby Dove..." Ian scanned the crowd as if he couldn't possibly fathom who Miss Ruby Dove might be.

"I am she," said Ruby, raising her hand.

Fina held her breath as she watched the two. Their eyes locked ever so momentarily. She knew from experience that they were both superb actors.

"Ah, Miss Dove. Mr Hayford tells me you and a Miss Aubrey Havelock—" Fina raised her hand, suppressing a grin. "—yes, that the two of you have an extensive résumé of private investigatory experience. Is it true?"

The pair nodded in unison.

Dot slammed her fist on the table and stood up. "How can we be certain this isn't another ruse or another attempt to murder us all in our beds? Who are you, anyway? You all could have set this up beforehand!"

Fina had to hand it to the woman. She was sharp. Much sharper than her obtuse brother.

Ian waved his hand. "No, you don't, Miss—"

"Miss Dorothy Synge, thank you very much," she replied.

"Miss Synge, yes, pleased to make your acquaintance. I'll admit you have no reason to believe anything I say. But at this point, you really don't have a choice, do you?" he said with a genuine smile. "So, in light of this duo's detecting skills, I propose to listen to their theories about what happened. Mr Belrose has been helpful, so I'd welcome his theories as well."

All of a sudden, the train lurched forward.

"We're moving!" cried Sophia in an uncharacteristic outburst.

Ian smiled. "Yes, I thought it only fair as a gesture of goodwill on my part. It will still be another eight hours before we reach Lausanne. The engine driver informed me there's treacherous weather ahead."

"Of course there would be," said Dot, twisting her lips into a sneer.

"*Gott* is good," pronounced Father Schweinsteiger, rocking back and forth.

"*Gott* has nothing to do with it, *Vater*," said Mrs Hartman. The two had already settled into a gentle squabbling-couple routine, despite an age difference of at least thirty years.

Everyone applauded and cheered. "This calls for a drink!" said Madeline, rising to her feet.

"*Mo-ther,*" said Dot. "Do sit down."

"I'll do nothing of the sort. It's time for a celebration, despite everything!"

"Don't you think a celebration is rather unseemly, Mother?" asked Ridgewell.

A flapping white object flew through the air. It hit Ridgewell squarely on the jaw.

"What the devil?" he said, rubbing his cheek as Ada's embroidery hoop fell to the floor.

All four feet and five inches of Mrs Hartman rose from her seat. *"Dummheit und Stolz wachsen auf einem Holz!"*

Father Schweinsteiger cleared his throat. "That translates as 'stupidity and arrogance grow from the same tree'."

"Ja!" said Ada. "You two children should have more respect for your mother. You've done nothing but mistreat her this entire journey. A crisis is no excuse to disrespect her."

Pixley clapped. Soon everyone had joined in – save the Synges. Dot glared at Ada. Ridgewell stared at his knees.

"Thank you, Mr Hayford," said Ian. He whispered into Laurent's ear. Laurent nodded. "It is indeed excellent news, dear passengers, that we are now moving," said Ian. "We've been sitting through an ordeal for a while, and I'm sure you have an appetite. Thanks to Maurice, Miss Dove and Miss Aubrey-Havelock, dinner only needs thirty minutes of preparation. I suggest everyone refresh themselves and prepare for dinner."

A bouncing energy filled the room, as if they had all just been invited to the ball. Everyone sprang up and flooded toward the doorway to the sleeping cars.

"Thank goodness," said Fina. "I need to change my clothes urgently. I'm suffocating in this jumper. Ready?"

"Definitely," said Ruby, even though her voice wavered.

They were the last ones to leave the room. As Fina expected, Ian whispered, "Ruby, do wait a minute."

"Go on, Feens, I'll catch you up soon," said Ruby, turning toward Ian in the empty lounge.

Fina smiled. "Be careful that no one spies you two," she giggled.

And though Ruby glared at Ian, neither of them paid any attention to Fina's words.

26

"Ah, that's much better," said Fina, flouncing down on Pixley's chair.

"I dunked my head in a basin full of cold water," said Pixley. "And I feel so much better for it."

"Braver than I am," replied Fina. "Here – would you care for a mint?"

"Yes, I need that too, even though I brushed my teeth at least ten times."

They sucked on their mints in companionable silence, staring out at the twilit mountains.

"Where's Ruby?"

"I'll give you three guesses," giggled Fina.

"I do hope those two are careful," said Pixley. "I don't want someone to spy on them."

"While we're waiting, do you want to share your theories of what, exactly, is going on?"

"Regarding Ian and Ruby?" he smiled.

"No, you goose, the murders. I know better than to ask you about what Ian is doing," said Fina.

"Well, these conversations are usually pointless without Ruby – no offence taken, I hope."

Fina stuck out her lower lip in a pout. She crossed her arms. "The problem is that Ruby knows the answer, but doesn't share it with me." She paused. "That's not fair to her, I suppose. I have just as much a chance to solve a murder as she does!"

"That's the spirit, Feens. Sometimes it seems pointless," he agreed, "because she always does reveal the solution in the end. But we can do it this time."

Pixley removed his reporter's notebook and scribbled across the top. He mouthed the words, "Suspects, motives, opportunity."

"Right," said Fina, hopping up from the bed. She realised she was unconsciously copying Ruby by pacing in small circles. "Let's proceed methodically, cabin by cabin."

Pixley waved his pencil up and down. "Splendid idea. First cabin after James's is Sophia Salazar's compartment."

"Sophia Salazar..." Fina said, twirling around when she reached the washstand to avoid a collision. "What do we know about her? Butter wouldn't melt in her mouth."

"You can say that again."

"And she's a famous author of naughty novels from Portugal."

"But didn't you tell me she met Raoul in Barcelona?"

"Of course, but that doesn't mean she doesn't travel. She must do a great deal of travelling as an author," she said, waving one finger in the air. "Hence her journey to Paris for a book signing."

"Any discernible motive or opportunity?" asked Pixley.

"Well, everyone had an opportunity to murder James and Neeya. As for the murder of Etienne, the only people who didn't have the opportunity were Miss Salazar and Mrs Hartman."

"So we can cross off Miss Salazar from the list of suspects?" asked Pixley as his tongue protruded from the corner of his mouth. He scribbled furiously.

"Well, I suppose we can eliminate Miss Salazar and Mrs Hartman as it seems entirely implausible that we have two murderers on board."

"But it is possible we have two murderers on board," said Pixley.

"How? Oh, I see what you mean," said Fina. "Accomplices. That's definitely a possibility, which is why we should keep those two on the list."

"Right," he said, drawing a line in the notebook. "Raoul is next."

"We know that his country of origin is rather vague, and he has an odd relationship with Miss Salazar."

"Any motive?"

"Hmmm…" said Fina.

"Feens," he said. "You're tapping your teeth like Ruby does when she's thinking."

"What?" she said, looking at her fingers as if they belonged to some other being. She giggled. "Well, I do need to take on the persona of the great detective if I want results!"

"Fair enough," he said. "I can't see any motive for Raoul to kill any of them, can you?"

"No, except perhaps Etienne. Might have something to do with Ridgewell?"

"Ridgewell Synge?" Pixley asked, as if there might be another. "What's it got to do with him?"

"Oh, Pixley," said Fina affectionately. "Some journalist you are. Haven't you seen the way they look at each other?"

Pixley chewed his pencil. "To be honest, Feens, I hadn't. Well, well … it's worth keeping in mind, at any rate. although I can't see how it fits in with the killings. I'll mark him as an outside possibility."

"Now on to Mrs Hartman. She didn't have the opportunity to murder Etienne, but she could have murdered James or Neeya."

"Why on earth would she do that?"

"I haven't a clue," admitted Fina. She didn't feel able to admit to Pixley that her prejudice against Ada's birthplace made the German woman seem suspect in her mind. There's something definitely peculiar about our sweet grandma, but I'm not sure what it has to do with any of the three murders."

"I agree."

"Next, we have the Synges. Oh my, what a family,"

"Couldn't agree more. I've had a bellyful of them already," said Pixley. "I feel sorry for Mrs Synge. She seems like a sweet enough person – I've often wondered how pleasant parents can produce such monstrous children."

"Ridgewell is particularly dreadful."

"And he hasn't any loyalty to his mother. It's hard for me to respect someone like that."

"Well, we aren't here to respect them, are we?"

"Touchy, touchy, Miss Ruby Dove."

Fina gave him a mock punch in the arm.

"We know little about the Synges, except they travelled to Cairo. That gives them a connection to Miss Arafa."

"Agreed," he said. "As for James and Etienne, however, there are no apparent associations, much less motives."

"Could be that those two murders were used to cover up the real crime, which was to target Neeya."

"Very clever, Feens. It's possible, but two murders? Seems like overkill," he said, his mouth opening into a wide 'O' as soon as he caught his unintentional pun. "Sorry."

"Yes, I agree. But we still can't eliminate them as suspects. The other odd thing is someone removed portraits from Ridgewell's sketchbook," said Fina.

"Ah, yes. You know, I had a little nose around the wastepaper basket after he tore up those sketches, while everyone was listening to Laurent in the lounge. Took it with me when I went to fetch Ian."

"Did you really! Pix, I take it all back – you are indeed a champion journalist. What have you discovered?"

Pixley's face lost its air of triumph. "Not much. I didn't have time to sit and piece them all together, and they were jolly finely shredded, too. But I did notice one with a horse and a riding crop. The other was one of the pyramids. That's it." He paused. "On to the governor. A real relic. In all senses of the word. Though I must say he tries his best to liven things up. I believe the only possible motive he had is again this connection to Egypt. I'd put him higher on the list of suspects over the Synges, given his past government posts. And the British government is anxious to quash the resistance."

"Yes," said Fina, smoothing her frizzy hair. "I agree. But somehow he seems improbable, doesn't he?"

"What do you mean?"

"I misspoke. I meant to say he seems improbable as a suspect, but I realise that his personality seems improbable, doesn't it? A little too hearty, if you know what I mean?"

"Mmmm... You may be right. But it doesn't make him a murderer, does it?"

"No, but I cannot see that anyone strikes me as a probable murderer on this train. Unless, of course, someone had murdered Dot."

"Lastly, we come to Felix Schweinsteiger. Now *there's* a character that seems improbable," said Pixley.

"You mean because of his last name? 'Pig climber' in German?" asked Fina.

"Is that what it means? Frankly, yes. But that alone wouldn't make me suspicious. No, it's that he had multiple passports and has a gambling problem. This would make him a prime target for extortion."

"So someone put the squeeze on him, as Americans say? Extortion?"

"That's a possibility. It makes him vulnerable."

"And yet from what I've observed at the bridge table, he's flush with cash. Not what you'd expect from someone under financial pressure." She flopped down on the bed next to Pixley. "So that leaves us with precisely nothing," she said disconsolately.

"No, I think we made some progress," said Pixley. "At least we know now we're not missing something obvious."

"Speaking of missing something, shouldn't Ruby have returned from the lounge by now?"

Pixley's eyebrows wiggled suggestively.

"No, really, joking aside, I think something is wrong."

~

RUBY STARED out of the window, arms crossed.

"I can only imagine what you think of me, Ruby," said Ian, remaining near the doorway.

"My grandmother told me that when you run with dogs, you should expect to be bitten by their fleas."

"That's a bit harsh, but I suppose I deserve it."

She spun round with her arms still crossed, but her jawline had softened. "Why are you putting us and the campaign in danger like this?" She paused. "No, what is infuriating is you didn't tell me about these planned shenanigans, but you told Pixley. Is this some sort of attempt to keep women in their place?"

He shook his head. "I can see why you'd think that, but you must believe that Pixley didn't know what I was doing, either. He only found out once I brought in Eustace to discuss our demands in the Caribbean."

"Our what?"

He held up his hands in mock surrender. "I'll explain it all to you later, I promise, but please know it is completely aligned with your goals." He sat down on a sofa, shoulders slumped. "I didn't tell you about the plan because I was afraid you'd get hurt."

"How is that different to being paternalistic? Why wouldn't you ask and let me make that decision?"

"You're right. I should have done that. I let my feelings get the better of my judgment, and I shouldn't let that happen when so many lives – including ours – are in the balance. I will learn my lesson."

Ruby's arms uncrossed. "Ian, you know how difficult it is for me to trust anyone, and when you pull colossal stunts like this, it sets me back years from trusting you completely."

"Years?"

"Well, let's say months."

Without looking up, he nodded at the floor. Then he bounced up off the sofa. "I know it will take time, and I'm willing to wait. And to rebuild your trust," he said, coming nearer. "Could I have a kiss if I tell you a plan where you're the star?"

"Hmmm ... perhaps."

"It will require you to go to the lavatory."

"Ian Clavering!"

He laughed. "No, no, let me explain. But first..." he said, moving in closer.

27

Fina glanced at the clock. "We would have noticed Ruby pass, since your door is open." She peered up and down the hallway. All she saw was Ricki dancing in and out of Raoul's cabin.

"Let me check the lavatory at our end of the sleeping car," said Fina, stepping out into the hall. "Pixley!" she hissed. "Come quickly!"

"What is it?" he said, nearly slipping in the doorway in his haste.

"The loo door is locked. And I already knocked a few times."

"Good lord. Not again," he cried, dashing off down the corridor. "I'll find Laurent for the key!"

Fina banged on the door. Then she cried, "Ruby! Ruby! Are you in there?"

She listened to the door as if she were a doctor

listening to a patient's breathing during a physical exam.

Finally, she heard a groan. It was Ruby's groan. Fina sighed and relaxed her shoulders, just an inch. At least she was alive.

Laurent appeared, skeleton key in hand. "*Voila.* Let me try this."

He wriggled the key in the lock and then tried another. Finally, the door burst open.

Ruby lay sprawled on the floor, moaning softly.

"Quickly, now. Move her to the bed," said Laurent. He and Pixley lifted her up gingerly and into her cabin. Fina sat down next to her friend and peered at the back of her head. Her hair was matted, but there wasn't any sign of blood. Fina heaved another sigh of relief.

Rapid footfalls approached. Ian poked his head through the doorway. "Oh my Lord. Ruby!" he cried, rushing over to the bed.

He kneeled on the floor while holding her hand. Though Fina was too worried to pay much attention to the scene, she smiled at the romantic tableau.

Ruby turned over to one side to face everyone, wincing as she did so.

Her eyes popped open unexpectedly. "Oof ... my head. Anyone have headache tablets?"

Pixley ran to his compartment.

"Can you speak?" asked Ian, laying his head on her hand.

"Mmmh ... I think so. I'm going to have quite a bump

in the morning. Fortunately, I'm hardheaded enough that the murderer couldn't kill me."

"Do you feel like you can tell us what happened?" asked Fina.

Ruby sat up. "Once I have those headache tablets, I'll be fine," she said as Pixley entered with the tablets and a glass of water.

"That's better." Ruby swallowed both tablets at once. "As for what happened to me, all I can remember is that I was in the lavatory, washing my hands. I had my back to the door. Then I felt the blow against the back of my head, but I lost consciousness. The murderer missed the mark, too, as they hit more of my neck than my head," she said, touching her neck.

"Of course," said Fina.

"Wait. Pixley – would you do me a favour and retrieve something from James's cabin? I hope it's still there," she said. Ruby whispered into Pixley's ear. Fina was slightly annoyed she hadn't been included in this secret.

Pixley toddled out and soon returned with a matchbox from James's compartment. Ruby shook it. It sounded empty.

"Good," she said. "Thank you."

Ian stared at her and shook his head but then said, "Right." He stood up and adjusted his suit. "It's time to wrap up this nonsense before someone else is injured. Fina – would you stay here with Ruby?"

"But Ian," said Ruby, taking another sip of water, "you cannot solve this without me present. You know that all too well."

Ian reluctantly agreed Ruby might join them all for dinner. Pixley and Laurent moved a settee from the lounge into the dining room so she could recline.

"You look divine, Ruby. Just like a queen with her court around her," said Fina, sitting next to her with her a plate of tarte flambée. Another plate sat next to her for Ruby, though Ruby said she wasn't hungry. The last time Fina had been coshed on the head, her first reaction had been to ask for toast and tea.

As the others filed in, everyone stared at Ruby, clearly perplexed by this latest turn of events. But they all had too much of an appetite to ask many questions. They nattered away about trivialities as if this were their first night on the train. Fina didn't blame them. That's how she'd cope as well.

The wine flowed, as did the cocktails. Even Laurent appeared a little less harassed after two glasses of wine. Sophia had dressed for the occasion in a bronze silk gown with a cross-the-neck cape.

Maurice and Julien had cleared away the dishes and began to serve coffee, port, and dessert. Laurent rose from his seat.

"May I have your attention, please," he said, padding toward Ruby. "I'm sure you're all puzzled about why Miss Dove is reclining on a settee in the dining room, though I suspect little can surprise you at this point in our journey. Someone assaulted Miss Dove an hour ago in the lavatory."

"How?" asked Dot.

"She was hit on the head," said Ian. "Fortunately, the murderer didn't account for Miss Dove's hardheadedness. Oh, and the murderer had atrocious aim," he said.

Fina watched as Ruby's eyes began to roll. But then she must have remembered she wasn't supposed to be familiar with Ian, so she restrained herself.

Ian continued. "We are also fortunate that someone was seen closing the lavatory door after the attack. That person must have been the murderer."

28

Gasps.

Did Ian really know? Or was this a bluff?

"So you know who the murderer is?" asked Eustace. "Well, out with it, man!"

"I'd like to make this worm squirm a little longer. Besides, there are loose ends we need to tie up before everything makes complete sense," said Ian. He waved a hand at Ruby. "Miss Dove, do you feel well enough to begin?"

Ruby nodded as she pulled herself a little more upright, wincing. "Thank you, Mr Rampton. This has indeed been a most perplexing case. I was completely at sea until after I was attacked. Let's review each murder in turn. I'll begin with the first, which wasn't a murder at all."

"What have you up your sleeve this time?" asked Pixley.

Fina giggled as Ruby withdrew the matchbox from her sleeve. "Why this, dear Pixley," she said, holding it up as if she were a magician about to perform a trick. She shook it. Silence. Then she opened it, and a folded slip of paper descended to the floor like one of the snowflakes outside the window. Fina bent over and picked it up.

"Please read it, Fina, if you wouldn't mind."

Clearing her throat, Fina began.

"Dear Fina, Pixley, and Ruby..."

Selkies and kelpies. Tears welled up, blurring her sight.

"I've been asked to do something I cannot do. It would put all of you in grave danger. If I were to accede to this request — no, demand — then one of you might die as a result. I cannot do that. Though I've searched for another way out, I cannot find one. If I do not follow these orders, then my family will suffer a great deal. If I do, then you three will suffer.

This is the only way out of this situation. Never blame yourselves for it.

Please forgive me,

James Matua"

Ada blew her nose. Sophia sniffed. Raoul covered his eyes with his handkerchief. Eustace took another swig of brandy.

"So it was suicide, after all?" asked Madeline.

Ruby nodded. "I suspected it might be, but only after the other murders occurred. I spotted this matchbox among James's belongings and thought it odd it was empty. James was clearly prepared for the journey because he had an ample supply of cigarettes. Then it dawned on me to search there, after I had figured out it was suicide, not murder."

"But why was Mr Matua drugged? Did someone not tamper with his chocolate box?" asked Laurent.

"There are two possibilities. The first is that James tried to kill himself by overdosing on sleeping tonic – which was unsuccessful. We found a half-full bottle of it in his cabin. The other possibility is he took a sleeping tonic because he couldn't face whatever it was he had to do."

"What about Neeya overhearing someone in the hallway? And then finding the pistol there?" asked Fina.

"I believe James dropped the pistol in the hallway before he jumped. I'm not sure why he'd do that."

Pixley said, "It might have been psychological. He had purchased the gun in Milan – and one can only surmise from his note that he was going to have to use it against one of us. Maybe he wanted to rid himself of it. To be pure when he..." He trailed off.

"Yes," said Ruby. "I believe that's the most likely scenario. Unfortunately for all of us – not to mention James – his suicide offered an opportunity to our murderer."

"How so?" asked Father Schweinsteiger.

"It all ties in to the second crime. Neeya's murder."

The room was perfectly silent. Fina could hear the wind howling around the icy peaks outside. A storm must be on its way.

"First, it is necessary to understand what happened and the character of the murdered person," said Ruby, glancing at Fina.

Fina had her notebook ready. Occasionally peering down at her notes, she said, "Neeya Arafa was an extraordinary scholar. The first woman to pass the law exam in Egypt, she was on her way to begin a PhD course in Brussels. On the morning of James's death, she heard a noise in the hallway – a 'thud' as she called it. When she peeked out into the corridor, she spotted what we now know was James's pistol in front of her compartment. She took the pistol and couldn't decide who to tell about it. She and Ruby formed a bond. Neeya told Ruby about the pistol while they were chatting in her cabin about the latest fashions," said Fina, letting out a sigh.

"That is how I came to possess a pistol in my clutch after Miss Arafa died," said Ruby. "It wasn't until later that I began to wonder if Miss Arafa supported an Egyptian resistance group."

"What do you mean?" asked Raoul with an air of innocence. "I'm a terrible dullard when it comes to world affairs."

"The Italian invasion of Ethiopia earlier this year consumed the attention of British politicians. Egyptian nationalists viewed this diversion – again – as an opportunity to resist British rule. I wondered if Miss Arafa were somehow connected to this story and was killed for that reason," said Ruby.

"Wouldn't the Synges be implicated, in that case?" said Fina, secretly enjoying accusing Dot and Ridgewell – not Madeline, though.

Ruby nodded. "They most certainly would. Would you three care to explain your real reason for being in Egypt?"

The family looked at one another. Madeline sighed. "Well, I suppose it will come out one way or another. It's true enough my husband was attached to the British embassy in Cairo. And that he died. But..."

Ridgewell continued. "But we're not Madeline's children," he said, staring at his knees.

Sophia nudged Raoul. "I told you there wasn't something right about that family." Raoul nodded.

"Is your real name Ridgewell Hinton, Mr Synge?" asked Ruby. "What I mean is, that story you told about not getting on with your father wasn't entirely true, was it? Your name really is Hinton, and it's not Madeline's maiden name, either."

Ridgewell's jaw dropped.

Dot tapped her fingers on the table. "It's true. We're using the family connection as cover to leave the country safely. But that is all. We had never met, much less heard of, Miss Arafa before this cursed train journey. Though she made us nervous because we thought she could be a spy."

"So you did have motives to kill her," said Ada from the corner of the lounge. Her embroidery had progressed into a mass of what appeared to be purple flowers but might have just as easily been a bunch of grapes.

"Do you work for the British government?" asked Ian, eyes narrowing.

"No, dear boy, we're not spies, if that's what you're thinking." Ridgewell chuckled at the very thought. "We're civil servants with connections back in Merry Old England. We found ourselves mixed up in a spot of trouble in Cairo, so we needed a safe passage out. This was the best option the embassy could concoct. Mrs Synge was already returning to London via *Train Blanc*, so joining her as family provided an easy cover."

Fina couldn't help herself. "Why did you decide to be so critical of Madeline, Dot?"

Dot's eyes flashed. "Perhaps I laid it on a bit thick, but I wanted it to be convincing that we were a family. Ridgewell was hopeless."

"*Quelle histoire,*" said Laurent. "But how does it relate to the murder?"

"The Synges were the only ones who seemed to have a real motive to murder Miss Arafa – that is, with intent to murder Miss Arafa specifically. I needed to confirm it before we proceeded," said Ruby.

"But we didn't – we didn't kill her! We barely even spoke to her. Oh, how can you say such dreadful things," said Dot, her voice rising ever higher in pitch.

"No," said Ruby gently, "I don't believe you did. Neeya's killer was someone else on board this train."

Silence. Ruby carried on. "I will say Mr Wistow did cross my mind as another suspect with a specific intent to murder Miss Arafa," she said.

The governor's moustache quaked. "Preposterous. Codswallop," he blustered.

"You have obvious connections to the British government. How can we be certain you weren't also negotiating on behalf of the government in your capacity as a former official?" asked Ruby.

"But, I've been in Italy for the past two months," he protested.

Fina held up two tickets. "It's true you were in Rome. But you also flew to Cairo for a week, didn't you?"

"As I told you before, for a bit of a vacation from Rome, my dear," he said, still blustering but wiping his forehead. "To see the pyramids."

"But surely that would take less than a week," said Fina.

Eustace crumpled, shrinking inside his shell like a turtle. "Well, it's true I went there to speak to British officials, but it was in an informal capacity. To advise them about, well, controlling the situation, as it were."

"And I bet you have plenty of experience with that, don't you, Governor?" sneered Pixley.

The governor ignored the jibe. "I assure you it was not clandestine in any way. Besides that, we have no evidence Miss Arafa was involved in the rioting."

"You're absolutely right, Mr Wistow. We needed to be sure," said Ruby.

"So you're saying that Miss Arafa was not victimised for her nationality. Then why in God's name was she killed?" asked Ian.

Ruby's shoulders slumped. "In fact, Mr Rampton," she said, looking straight at Ian, "the truth is even more distressing."

29

Ruby took a breath and plunged on. "Miss Arafa was never meant to be a victim," she said. "I suspect the killer planned on committing their own, unrelated crime further along in our journey, or when they arrived at their destination. Either way, the chain of events sparked by James's disappearance offered them a chance to distract us from their purpose." She paused, smoothing her hair. "If we examine the tragic murder of Miss Arafa, we will begin to understand how this elaborate charade unfolded. In fact, it was my reflection on our game of charades that sparked the idea of a diversion."

"You mean Miss Arafa's death was nothing more than a diversion?" asked Pixley.

Ruby nodded. "Of sorts."

"Well, that's awful," said Madeline, scandalised. Her

hand flew up to her throat. "What I mean is, it's dreadful no matter how you view it, but for someone's death to be a mere distraction, well..."

"I agree," said Ruby. "This was a dastardly crime. But the crucial thing to realise here is that it wasn't meant to be that way. The murderer is not quite as devilish as you're imagining, Mrs Synge."

"Oh, piffle!" cried Madeline. "To take the life of a young woman like that, with such bright prospects – why, the man must be nothing short of a monster."

"But you see, that was never the plan." Ruby sighed and rubbed her temples. The head wound was sapping her patience. "Let me go into it all more closely. The important point is the murderer must have overheard my conversation with Neeya about how she got hold of James's gun."

"Why is that important?" asked Eustace.

"Because the perpetrator realised that it would be greatly to their advantage if we all believed there was already a killer on board the train, with a separate agenda. If everyone thought James had been murdered – and indeed, it's possible the murderer believed that themselves – then it would be logical for Miss Arafa to be the next victim, because she might have observed something that would incriminate James's killer."

It was Dot's turn to be outraged. "My mother is right. To kill someone for such a scheme is monstrous!"

"Ah, but they didn't," Ruby replied. "At least, they never meant to. Neeya's death was an accident."

"*Ach du meine Güte!*" exclaimed Father Schweinsteiger. The others simply stared.

"At least, it was meant to be an *attempted* murder," said Ruby. "The culprit saw an opportunity to draw attention away from the crime that they themselves planned to carry out not long afterwards. If Neeya was doped with harmless pills – enough to make her noticeably ill, but not enough to poison her – it would look as though someone was trying to cover their tracks following James's death. That was the murderer's plan: a charade to distract us, with Neeya an unwitting player in the game. She was never meant to be a genuine victim."

Ridgewell let out a low whistle. "Our murderer is quite clever, aren't they, Miss Dove?"

Ruby smiled at him, but it was a smile with too many teeth. A warning?

"Miss Arafa drank copious amounts of hot beverages, particularly coffee. It was easy to dissolve the pills in such a strong-tasting drink."

"But what about the cyanide?" said Ian.

"Mhhmmm," said Ruby, sipping her own glass of water. "That was a tragic mistake – one the murderer could never have foreseen. As far as he or she knew, those pills that went into Neeya's coffee were nothing more than sleeping tablets."

Pixley leaned forward. "I still don't understand," he

said, drumming his fingers on the table-top as if to pin down the solution. "How did all this come about? And who was responsible?"

Ruby gave him a small smile. "As far as opportunity, it was fairly obvious any of us could have slipped the pills into Neeya's coffee."

"We were all moving about while playing charades," said Raoul. "It would be easy for the murderer."

"Who suggested charades?" asked Dot.

Heads swivelled around the room. "I believe it was Father Schweinsteiger, wasn't it?" asked Ridgewell.

"No, Wellie, it was Governor Wistow," said Dot, gazing at the still dazed figure in the chair by the window. His head looked like a white silhouette against the night outside. He passed a hand over his forehead in puzzlement. "It would be something I would do, but I cannot remember…"

"It's hard to say whether it mattered," said Ruby. "The murderer sought out any opportunity, so it's possible Mr Wistow made the suggestion innocently."

"So you're saying we all had the opportunity to poison – or try to poison – Miss Arafa," said Dot. "Brilliant. That leaves us where?"

Ruby ignored Dot's tone. Fina agreed it was best not to feed the animals.

"More to the point, dash it, anyone could have slipped that pillbox into my pocket!" declared Ridgewell.

At that, Ruby whirled around. Fina had seen that look on her face before. She had caught the scent.

"But they didn't, did they, Mr Synge – or should I say Mr Hinton? That was your own pillbox, in your own pocket, filled to bursting with your own pills. And most of them were perfectly innocuous quick-dissolve sleeping tablets, as you'd had us believe. But there was one pill that was different. It was distinct from the others only subtly, perhaps with a groove across the top, or a small imprinted logo. Nothing that you would notice if you didn't know what to look for, or feel for with your fingertip. And the murderer never did notice it. They tossed a handful of tablets in Miss Arafa's hot coffee, thinking to make her seem like an intended victim. Never knowing that one of those tablets contained a lethal dose of cyanide."

Gasps. All eyes locked on Ridgewell. He fidgeted uncomfortably, his urbane self-assurance rapidly draining away.

"Is this true, Mr Hinton?" demanded Ian. "Can you explain yourself?"

"Balderdash, old man," said Ridgewell. "Absolute bosh. This young lady has – er – let her imagination get the better of her."

Ian glanced at Ruby and she gave him the tiniest nod of her head. He turned back to Ridgewell with the assurance of one who has just seen incontrovertible proof.

"Mr Hinton, I'm familiar with those pill-cases and

their contents. There's only one class of person who carries such a thing, and that is an employee of the Secret Service: someone high up enough to be a security risk if they should fall into the hands of the enemy. You had better admit that you are one such, sir – now that your suicide pill has been used to bring about the death of an innocent woman."

Clever of Ian, Fina thought. Surely Ridgewell will have the decency to come clean now. And so it proved. He heaved a sigh and addressed Ian directly, avoiding the shocked stares of the rest of the party.

"It's true, I was under deep cover in Egypt," he admitted. "I was there to infiltrate student groups to see if we could find out what their next moves might be. I couldn't directly infiltrate, of course, so my job was to recruit informants. Madeline and Dorothy here are not to be blamed, mind you. They were going back to Blighty in any case, since the situation in Cairo is so unstable, and they were enlisted to provide cover for me. A family travelling together is less suspicious than a single man."

Madeline could contain herself no longer. "And you had that cyanide pill with you all that time, in the pill-box? Why, Ridgewell, we might have taken it in all innocence – and there was enough poison there to kill any of us!"

"Yes," he said levelly. "Yes, there was."

"So you're not a high-level spy, then," Pixley asked Dot, a hint of a twinkle in his eye.

"Not remotely," she told him. "In fact, I'm a decoder. You know, for secret messages."

A slight tittering among the passengers broke the tension. Outside the train carriage, a flurry of raindrops whipped against the window. Ada poured herself another cup of tea and Fina seized the chance to help herself to a biscuit. All kept their faces turned away from Ridgewell. Really. These spies and their careless way with poison pills. As if she needed another reason to dislike the British government.

Finally, Ruby cleared her throat. "If I may be allowed to continue ... we still have not got to the bottom of this case. We've yet to consider the most crucial aspect: the murder of Etienne Durand. The real target."

30

Ruby looked at Pixley, who bobbed his head and took up the baton. "Mr Etienne Durand was a French diplomat returning from negotiations with the Italian government in Rome We are not aware of the nature of these talks, but we surmise they may have something to do with Italy and Ethiopia," he said, waving his hand as if swatting a fly. "But the subject of these negotiations is irrelevant. What is important is he was travelling to Paris for high-level negotiations with the Soviets about the current turmoil in Europe. Particularly with regards to the situation in Germany. So the question is, who would want those talks to fail?"

"Well, someone involved with the German government, naturally," said Sophia.

All eyes turned on Ada and Felix.

Felix leapt out of his chair. "Just because I speak

German, you accuse me? Me! A man of the cloth! How dare you? And besides, I am Swiss, not a German national. There is a great difference," he said, holding one finger in the air as if he were calling his flock to order.

Ada smiled and hummed, continuing to stab the needle through her embroidery.

Raoul said, "And you, Mrs Hartman, have you anything to say for yourself?"

Fina caught her breath. Would this be the moment when Ada declared her allegiance to the fascists who had such a hold on her home town, Braunschweig?

Ada set down her embroidery as if Raoul were an irritating child who would only go away if she paid attention to him. "*Ja,* I am a German citizen," she said, eyes fixing on Fina. "And I can tell by Miss Aubrey-Havelock's countenance you understand why Braunschweig is significant. But I want to have nothing to do with those filthy thugs. In fact, that is why I am travelling a circuitous route to leave the country."

"Is that because of the Nuremberg laws – and you're not classified as what do they call it? Aryan?" asked Sophia.

"No, *mein Schatz,*" she said, picking up her embroidery again. "I am what I believe is called a 'homosexual' in English."

Silence.

"That's why I'm travelling to France. England has

horrific laws about that, and Spain, well, is turning from progressive to archaic on the subject."

"And many other subjects as well," said Sophia.

"There's another reason though, isn't there?" asked Pixley.

"My, you are clever, Mr Hayford."

Pixley turned to Felix. "Father, how much money have you lost during this journey, playing cards with Mrs Hartman?"

Felix rose again to the challenge then tried to sit back down. But he misjudged the distance and he and his chair toppled over. Laurent and Julien rushed over to help him to his feet.

"I – I – I –" he stammered.

"10,000 francs and 5,000 lira," replied Ada.

"She must have been the one who cheated at cards!" yelled Dot.

Ignoring Dot's outburst, Ruby continued, "Now we arrive at the reason for the behaviour of both Mrs Hartman and Father Schweinsteiger. Father, you gamble a great deal. And lose a great deal, do you not? And you had a curious number of receipts in your compartment as well."

He looked down at his shoes. The laces were untied.

"Yes," he sighed. "I went to Monte to try my hand at the casinos. I'm afraid I got into a great deal of debt. My creditors followed me. I thought I'd be safer travelling via the *Train Blanc* rather than a regular train back to

Switzerland." Then he threw his shoulders back, as if to brave a storm. "I collect other people's receipts so I can submit them to the archdiocese for reimbursement – to help offset my debts," he said, pausing. "It's for the good of everyone that I continue as a priest."

There's someone with a high opinion of himself, thought Fina.

"But how could you afford tickets on *Train Blanc*?" asked Raoul.

"You'd be surprised how easy it is to get a loan when you're a priest," said Felix.

"What about your German passport?" asked Dot.

"My mother was German, and we lived in Germany for a short time when I was a child," he said.

"And the Russian literature?" asked Raoul. "You must be a spy!"

"I just enjoy Russian literature," Felix said, shaking his head sadly. "Is that a crime?"

Turning away from Felix, Sophia asked, "What's this about Ada? What's her second reason for fleeing Germany?"

"From what I understand, the Nazis have a no-tolerance policy toward anyone they perceive to be engaged in subversive or criminal activity," said Ruby. "Isn't that right, Mrs Hartman?"

"Yes," she sighed, stabbing her needle viciously into the cloth. "Although I am not a criminal. I detest this term. I am an artist! But they do not look too kindly on confidence artists."

"Well, well," said Ridgewell with a smirk. "Little Mrs Hartman is a confidence trickster." Fina wanted to kick Ridgewell but he was too far away.

"Knew it," muttered Dot under her breath, looking smug.

Ada patted Felix on the arm. "I'm sorry, dear, but you were such an easy target. I couldn't help myself. I didn't realise you were that badly off."

Felix blinked at Ada's hand on his arm, as if it were a spider creeping toward his face. His eyes narrowed as he lifted his face toward her. "*Teufel*," he spluttered, sweeping Ada's hand off his arm.

Ada shrugged. "I'll return my winnings to you."

His lips began to move but if he were saying something, Fina couldn't hear it. He nodded and drained a glass of water in one gulp. The glass hit the table with a thump, apparently signalling this embarrassing public exchange was at an end.

Ruby took the floor once again. "As you can see by these many passenger stories, trains are perfect for escaping a person or a situation. Especially luxury trains. Train officials are careful to bend to your every whim and rarely question you about much of anything. Passports can be faked, and police don't generally stop the *Train Blanc*. So escape was the theme of this journey." She paused and slowly fastened her gaze on Sophia and Raoul. "Miss Salazar and Mr Lapointe?"

Raoul shifted in his seat and rubbed the back of his neck. Sophia stared Ruby down.

"Fina pointed out that Mr Lapointe had an accent which Mr Durand couldn't identify at first. Then he determined later it was Parisian. That was odd enough, but then we also noted that Mr Lapointe acted as if he had never been to Paris before," said Ruby.

"Meaning Mr Lapointe is not French?" gambled Ian.

Raoul's Adam's apple bobbed up and down like a lift in a busy office building.

"Raoul's behaviour as a secretary struck me as bizarre from the first," said Ruby. "He appeared to be involved in a relationship with Miss Salazar – which was plausible – but then suddenly changed to be interested in Ridgewell here," she pointed at the visibly sweating Ridgewell. "And Miss Salazar wasn't the least bit concerned about it. Indeed, there seemed to be a blossoming romance between her and Mrs Synge," she said, glancing at Madeline, who didn't appear to be the least bit worried about the claim.

"I am an erotic fiction author," drawled Sophia. "I practise what I preach, unlike other people," she said, staring at Father Schweinsteiger. He had the decency to appear abashed.

Ruby nodded. "Yes, it's not that in and of itself which was peculiar. It's only when you consider that in combination with the apparently fake identity of Mr Lapointe, along with the real reason you're travelling to Paris. Remember the list of items from the search of the compartments? Raoul had a photo of a young woman taken in Tarragona in Spain," Ruby paused,. "With a rifle. That's an unusual enough sight that it made me remember it. Who was that woman, Raoul?"

He sighed, glancing over at Sophia. Sophia shrugged. "That's my sister," said Raoul. "She's joined an anarchist women's collective because men dominate so many leftist groups. Well, they're organising and preparing – including military training – for whatever is coming next in Spain. She's very brave, and I'm afraid I'm not. She told me I had to leave for my own safety – that I was under threat because of her political activities. Since we have the same last name, I changed mine and pretended to be French as my mother was French. I knew the language so it wasn't that difficult a change to make."

"And why are you travelling with Miss Salazar?" asked Ruby.

"I really am her secretary. We have agreed to part ways once we arrive in Paris, however."

Ruby looked over at Sophia as if to signal her to confirm this statement.

Sophia stubbed out a cigarette as if she were digging a hole in the ashtray. "I am who I say I am, but I'm fleeing both Portugal and Spain because I am an erotic fiction writer. Supposed deviant sexual behaviour – all lumped into one category of perversion – was tolerated in Spain for many years. But with the new regime coming into power, that has all changed. As for Portugal, there have been laws on the books since the 1880s. I had to escape to a country which would be more forgiving of my proclivities." She paused, sipping her wine. "And this was not simply so I could continue to write. Another famous poet has just been killed for having these proclivities, despite what the opposition might claim."

Heads nodded slowly, taking in yet another revelation.

Dot tapped her fingers again on the table. They sounded remarkably similar to the hail pelting the train carriage. "Haven't we left out a few suspects?" asked Dot. "What about Monsieurs Belrose, Gaudin and Paquet?"

"Who?" demanded Governor Wistow. "There's no one aboard with those names."

Fina could barely keep the contempt out of her voice. "The train staff, of course." He subsided back into his easy chair.

"Perhaps, but I have yet to fathom a motive for any of them – does anyone else know anything?" asked Ruby.

Maurice scratched at his teeth with a toothpick. Julien crossed one arm over another but then dropped them. He shuffled his feet. Laurent smoked a cigarette, watching Ruby out of the corner of his eye.

Fina's stomach tensed. Should she say she had

noticed Julien fiddling about in Etienne's compartment? He was a nice boy and she didn't want to get him in trouble. On the other hand, there might be a perfectly good explanation.

"Ah, ur, I have something to say," said Fina, twisting the belt of her frock around her finger. "I saw Julien rummaging around in Etienne's cabin after he died. And after we were all to go to the lounge," she whispered.

Julien dropped his cigarette on the floor. As he scooped it up, Laurent patted him on the shoulder. "Do not worry, Julien. All will be well."

After a quick glance at Ian, Laurent adjusted his uniform and licked his lips. He called out in French, in a ringing voice: "You may come in now."

31

"What the devil?"

"*Gott in Himmel!*"

"*Mon Dieu!*"

"*Dios mío!*"

There, in the doorway to the lounge, stood Etienne Durand.

"I knew it!" yelled Pixley, stamping his foot.

As Fina stared open-mouthed at Etienne, she noticed he looked more well-rested than everyone else in the lounge. He had performed some sort of magic on his suit so it appeared as pressed and clean as it had when he first entered the train. One corner of his mouth lifted in a mischievous grin.

"I regret any inconvenience our charade caused for anyone," said Etienne, waltzing toward the drinks tray. He poured himself a healthy dose of brandy.

Objections, exclamations and recriminations erupted.

Laurent waved both hands downward to call for silence. When that failed, he removed his whistle and blew it. The piercing noise certainly prompted everyone into hushed silence. Everyone's mouths stood frozen in mid-sentence like Edvard Munch's painting of *The Scream*.

Fina glared at Ruby. "You knew, didn't you?!" she hissed.

Ruby nodded sadly. "If it makes you feel any better, we didn't tell Pixley, either." Pixley looked venomously at Ruby and then at Ian.

Laurent glanced at Ian. "It was the idea of Mr Rampton," he said, "and though it took a while for me to apprehend the wisdom of the plan, I was persuaded – eventually. Julien and I, we had the pleasure of looking after Mr Durand."

So that was what Julien had been doing in Etienne's cabin. Fina felt a trifle guilty for having suspected the forthright young man.

"But, but why?" blabbered Eustace.

Ian, who had been standing near the doorway for the entire sequence of events, shifted his weight. "I suppose it's my turn to explain myself. Then everything else should fall into place," he said, taking a glass of brandy from Etienne.

Etienne slapped Ian on the back. "The man is a

genius, absolute genius," he said. Fina glanced at Ruby. She had never seen such a singular combination of pride and jealousy mixed on someone's face.

"My purpose in diverting the train wasn't what you might have thought – to rob you all, or to prevent Mr Durand from reaching Paris in time for his important meeting." He paused. "Quite the opposite. It was to save Mr Durand from certain death should he reach Lausanne."

"But why did you insist on talking to Governor Eustace first?" asked Father Schweinsteiger.

"That's a matter between myself and the governor, which doesn't involve the murder. Let's say it was a side benefit of this journey we all took together."

"Pardon my basic question, Mr Rampton," said Ridgewell, "But why should you care about Mr Durand's safety? And why would you care enough to take such a great personal risk to yourself?"

Ian paused, taking another sip of brandy. "I'm afraid I cannot reveal who I work for, but let's say I had information an assassination was going to occur. And from my employer's perspective, Etienne Durand is the only person in the French government who has a chance of convincing the Italian government to halt its invasion of Ethiopia."

"Couldn't you find another way of stopping him, rather than going to all this trouble?" asked Dot.

"Believe me, this was the last resort. My other

schemes to divert him from this journey utterly failed. I also knew that not only would assassins be lying in wait in Lausanne, but in all likelihood there was an assassin on this train."

"The most devilish thing about it all is that I booked the *Train Blanc* because I thought it would be the safest way to travel," said Etienne, shuddering. Then his cheerful countenance returned.

"Without the intelligence-gathering and deductions of one Miss Ruby Dove," said Ian, bowing toward her, "and the bravery of Pixley Hayford and Fina Aubrey-Havelock, I would never have arrived at the truth of who was targeting Mr Durand." He swung his glass in Ruby's direction. "Would you like to take it from here, Miss Dove?"

Ruby grinned, looking placated by this gesture. "Why thank you, Mr Rampton. Yes, I suspected something was peculiar about the murder of Mr Durand. But it was not until Mr Rampton informed me of his scheme that my hunch was confirmed."

"Wait a moment," said Ridgewell. "I don't understand why Mr Durand had to be 'fake' murdered in the first place – am I missing an important element of this story?"

Ian cleared his throat and opened his mouth. But Ruby was too quick for Mr Ian Clavering. "What better way to protect someone from imminent death than to pretend they're already dead?"

Heads bobbed slowly.

"Besides that, it had the added effect of completely throwing the murderer off their guard. What's more, as soon as they thought I knew Mr Rampton here, and that I had special detective skills—"

"Which you do," interjected Pixley.

"Thank you, Mr Hayford. So I became the bait. The murderer had already been thrown into a tailspin about Mr Durand's death. I'm certain that at first they must have felt elated that someone else had committed the crime for them. And I'm sure they also hoped that person would be implicated in the murders of Mr Matua and Miss Arafa."

"Deuced complicated," murmured Eustace.

"Yes, it was, rather. We leveraged the complacency caused by Mr Durand's fake murder to provoke the murderer. It was clear they'd be in serious trouble, once we got to Lausanne, if their secret was discovered, and so there was every chance they'd do something rash to protect themselves. We laid a trap by insinuating I knew something important," replied Ruby. "By staying behind to speak to Mr Rampton here, I made the murderer very nervous, particularly because I'd had earlier interactions with Miss Arafa. The murderer had no way of knowing whether I held back important information about our conversation that day."

"We knew the murderer would try to assault Miss Dove and so I followed her and hid to watch her when she went into the lavatory," said Ian, wiping his brow and then his mouth. "And I was almost..." He faltered, peering at Ruby like a lost dog.

"What Mr Rampton is saying is that unfortunately the murderer almost succeeded in bumping me off. Fortunately, Mr Rampton was near enough to scare them away," said Ruby, involuntarily touching the back of her head. She winced.

"So?" Raoul asked. "Who is it?

32

"You," said Ruby, pointing across the room.

Fina gasped.

"I?" Sophia fluttered a hand over her décolletage.

"You, Sophia," repeated Ruby. "Fina – our political historian – reminded me that the Portuguese prime minister's name is António de Oliveira Salazar."

"What of it?" said Sophia, unimpressed. "It's a common name."

"It is common, but then I began to contemplate your profession and the Salazar government more carefully. That government is deeply conservative and would certainly not be friendly to someone who writes erotic literature."

"That's why I left. To be honest, though I do have this author event in Paris, I'm not sure I'll return home," Sophia said, taking a long drag on her cigarette.

"Be that as it may, have patience while I explain thought and word associations in my mind."

"Wait a moment," said Fina, straightening up. "Salazar is a Basque name, isn't it? We've been studying the history of Spain and particularly the Basque nationalists."

"Precisely. Remember her insistence ordering a Basque dish?" Ruby said to Fina. "And then how Maurice complained foreigners insisted on ordering dishes related to their national cuisine?"

Fina nodded. "That is true. Maurice was upset."

Ruby continued. "So what if Sophia Salazar were Basque? Given recent political turmoil, she would have even more reason to leave. The fact she associated with Raoul – whose sister is a leftist of a sort – meant there might be a connection."

"Yes, yes," said Sophia. "Even if that's true – my father was Basque – what does it matter?"

Ruby ignored her comment. "Once I realised someone was trying to assassinate Etienne, I had to ask myself why. It was obvious – to cause a different outcome of French-Soviet talks. The purpose of assassinating him could not be only to stall the negotiations. If that were the case, it would be much easier to divert him so he wouldn't arrive in time," she said, pausing. "Mr Durand was the target, not the negotiations themselves. Therefore, there was something special about Mr Durand."

"I am quite special, if I do say so myself," said Etienne, who looked like the cat who got the cream.

Pixley held up his hand as if Ruby were a school teacher. "When I interviewed Mr Durand, he told me he had special relationships with several Italian and Soviet officials. He complained of his weakling assistant minister, Pierre Maurin."

Ruby took over again. "Pixley told me about the interview with Mr Durand, and I asked myself the following question. Who would replace Mr Durand if he were assassinated?"

"Pierre Maurin," said Fina.

"And that would advantage whom in the talks? The answer is the Soviets. It would be much easier to deal with an ineffectual diplomat – and gain maximum advantage in these talks to prevent German expansion."

Sophia's eyes flickered. She lit another cigarette.

"Are you saying Miss Salazar works for the Soviets?" asked Dot.

"That's my best guess," said Ruby. "It dovetails with her story. Whatever she says, I have a feeling she is involved with the Basque movement. I'm certain they view the Soviets as potential allies, especially given the incredibly volatile situation in Spain at the moment. Let me be clear, I am not saying they are *allies*, but they may have mutual interests."

"*Mein Schatz*, you do have a *fantastische* brain," exclaimed Ada, who had set aside her embroidery.

Ruby's only answer was to smooth her hair.

Laurent and Ian leaned over Sophia, ready to pounce.

But Sophia was too quick for the both of them. In a flash of silk and pearls, she had run to the door. From her clutch, she removed James's little pistol and waved it around the lounge.

"How did you steal that pistol?" asked Pixley in amazement.

"Never mind. It doesn't matter," she said, her eyes narrowing on her target. She pointed the gun at Ruby.

Fina's lips tingled as she held her breath.

Sophia faced Ruby, so she couldn't spot Ian loping slowly toward her like a jaguar.

He pounced, sending the gun flying across the lounge.

"¡*Déjame ir!*" she exclaimed, struggling from his grip.

"Ow!" screeched Ian.

Sophia had bitten his hand.

She slipped through the doorway.Ian, followed by the rest of the passengers, dashed after her.

But it was too late.

The exit door already hung open.

33

———

The train chugged into Lausanne train station, weary and exhausted from the long journey. Snow-covered mountains to their left loomed up over Lake Geneva while the merry red roofs of downtown popped up like little mushrooms out of the snow. Fina had expected an army of Swiss police to be waiting for their arrival as if they were royalty.

Instead, she spied one lonely police officer amongst the train crew and passengers at the station. She looked over at Ruby, who sat patiently with her hands crossed over her handbag in her lap.

"I thought there would be a horde of police waiting for a train with two deaths that had occurred on the journey," said Fina.

"I expect they haven't any idea about all that has

occurred over the past few days. They may only know we were held up on that bridge – not that there was intrigue aboard."

As the train came to a complete halt, Fina's stomach tightened. "What should we do when they want to question us?"

"Remember, Etienne will speak to them first. We'll follow his lead and tell them what happened, minus our own activities – as well as Ian's."

Julien saluted the police officer outside their window. After speaking a few moments, the police officer pointed at the carriage as if to board. Julien nodded his approval.

After some foot-stomping, presumably to remove snow, they heard footsteps approach their cabin.

Tap, tap.

"Police."

The door slid back before Ruby or Fina could reply.

Ruby and Fina nodded. Ruby clutched her bag. Fina clutched her stomach.

The officer tipped his hat. "*Police de Lausanne.* You speak English?" The man looked remarkably like Charlie Chaplin.

"Are you ill?" he asked, pointing at Fina's stomach.

Fina looked down at her stomach. "Oh, no, just hungry."

He smiled and flicked his wrist as he glanced at his

watch. "We will provide food at the station. But you understand we must go to the station?"

They nodded.

"But you must stay here first."

He hesitated, staring at Ruby just a moment too long. He flung his head to the right and marched down the corridor.

After a few moments, Pixley popped in.

"Aren't you supposed to stay in your compartment?" asked Ruby.

"Probably," he said as he lit a cigarette. The odour of the smoke rapidly became unbearable.

Fina opened the window. "Sorry. I'm not sure why, but the smoke is bothering me."

Ruby gave her a wry smile. "Me too. It's because we have an appetite."

Pixley looked down at his cigarette as if it had magically appeared between his fingertips. He stubbed it out in the ashtray. "Sorry. I'm famished, too. Do you think they'll have sandwiches and tea at the station?"

"Well, our police friend said something about food."

Fina sat bolt upright. "Wait a moment. Where's Ian? Wasn't he in your compartment? How on earth will Laurent explain why we had a passenger who didn't have a ticket or an assigned compartment?"

Leaning over to the window, Pixley pointed at someone walking off the platform in the distance.

Toward the lake rather than the town. "See that? It's Ian."

"I told him to do it," said Ruby. "He fussed at first but decided it was the best option. If he were to be found on the train, there would be too many loose ends to tie up for the police and suspicion would undoubtedly fall on us. Particularly Pixley," she said, sighing. "It took a good hour to convince Ian last night, but he finally agreed, once I told him he was putting the rest of us in danger."

"Too right," said Pixley. "But you know Ian's weakness is his pride. He felt like sneaking off the train meant he was shirking his responsibility."

Ruby nodded.

"Where was I during this discussion?" asked Fina, trying not to be hurt about being left out.

"Don't you remember you fell asleep right after you had your hot cocoa?" asked Ruby.

Fina jumped up and stared at both of them in turn. "Did – did – did one of you put sleeping powder in my cocoa?"

Ruby and Pixley laughed uncontrollably. Pixley's chin shook, and Ruby's handbag slid onto the floor as she covered her mouth.

"We'd never do such a thing, Feens," said Ruby, dabbing her eyes. "You were exhausted. So was I—"

"But at least you had an incentive to stay awake," said Pixley as he winked at Ruby.

Footsteps pounded in the corridor.

"What is all this noise?" demanded Charlie Chaplin. Without waiting for an answer to his apparently rhetorical question, he continued, "We will go now. Follow me."

34

———

The Lausanne police station, housed in a gothic building, loomed up before them. Once they entered, Fina twitched her nose at the distinct odour of wood smoke. And coffee. The bright lights of the hallways made her squint and cower, unlike the single buzzing lightbulbs of the police stations she had 'visited' at home.

Charlie Chaplin opened a door and motioned to Pixley to go inside. Next, he showed Ruby and Fina to a room across the hallway. A tray of sandwiches and coffee sat on the gleaming table inside. Fina didn't need to be told twice – and neither, apparently, did Ruby. They descended on the sandwiches like hungry ravens.

"Mmhh ... thank goodness," said Ruby as she munched on her sandwich with sips of coffee in between.

"'Thank goodness' is right," sighed Fina through a full mouth. She finished her sandwiches and then sipped her coffee. It was delicious. Even without anything extra in it.

Their cosy meal was not to last.

The door swung open and in marched a man in a brown overcoat and brown fedora. He was tall, untidy, and reeked of cigarettes. There was something distinctly familiar about the way he entered the room.

The sound of his voice explained everything. "Good morning, ladies," he said, taking off his hat and spinning a chair around backwards to sit in it.

He was English.

Ruby's coffee cup clattered on its saucer. Her hand flew up to one side of her face as if the gesture would hide her. Quickly, she forced her hand back into her lap. Fina sat at such an angle she could see Ruby's hands in her lap. Fortunately, the Englishman could not. They were quaking.

Watching Ruby's reaction caused a rush of anxiety from Fina's stomach to her ears. An instant headache. Fina had never seen Ruby this unnerved.

The man sat opposite Ruby, staring at her. Then his mouth curved into a terrifying smile. Even in the midst of the horror, Fina was reminded of the wolf and Little Red Riding Hood.

A sharp pain shot through her leg. Looking down, she saw Ruby had clawed her nails into her thigh. Fina could only interpret this as a message she should take the lead. Well, she'd do her best.

Fina smoothed her hair. "Hello, are you a visiting policeman?" It was the only thing she could think of to say. She smoothed her skirt. Noticing she unconsciously mimicked Ruby's habits when under pressure, Fina hoped it would make her appear calmer on the outside than the wreck she was on the inside.

The man turned to Fina as if he just noticed she was in the room. "Yes, Miss Aubrey-Havelock, you could say I'm visiting from London."

Fina gulped. He had said her name as if he were familiar with her – it rolled off his tongue.

"We're on our way back to London. That is if we can ever get there." Yes, prattling on was her best option, she decided. "We had these dreadful train difficulties – as I'm sure you know – and are late getting into Paris. We've definitely missed our train from Paris. But I'm sure they'll be able to—"

"Miss Aubrey-Havelock. Please," he said, loosening his red tie. "Don't play the innocent with me. You and Miss Dove here know exactly why I've come to question you."

Ruby smoothed her hair. "I'm afraid we don't know, ah – what is your name, please?"

"Inspector Hodsell. Scotland Yard," he said as he rummaged around in his pockets. He removed a badge and handed it to Ruby.

Ruby took the badge as if it were a dead rat and examined it gingerly. She let it drop on the table. "Thank you, Inspector Hodsell. Now, to continue. You believe we know why you're here? The only reason I can fathom is you're English, and we're English. Is my assumption incorrect?"

There was that smile again. Fina had the urge to reach across the table and slap him.

"I'm certain you know why I'm here, Miss Dove. But let's leave aside the guessing games for now," he said, pulling out a small notebook and pencil. He licked the tip and began to scribble. "Now," he leaned forward. "Tell me all about James Matua."

Ruby rubbed her nose. "James Matua was a fellow student at Oxford. Fina, here, became acquaintances with him as they were both students of political history. James was younger than us and tended to follow us around like a lost puppy, didn't he, Fina?" she asked, looking at Fina with the 'affirm-the-inspector' look.

"Oh, yes. A lost puppy is how I would describe it. Poor James was really a lost soul, now that I think about it more. He was from New Zealand, and he often spoke of his family – particularly his mother. You must have seen that in the suicide note he left, Inspector?"

The inspector looked a little taken aback but nodded. "Yes, I've read the letter. It's not addressed to anyone, though, which I find odd," he said, removing a folded sheet of paper from his pocket. "You see here?"

he said, unfolding the paper and pointing to the edges. "The letter has a jagged edge. Can you explain that? It looks as though someone tore the edges."

Ruby took the letter from the inspector and studied it, frowning. She held up a finger in triumph. "James had an odd habit. I suppose you might call it a nervous tic, Inspector Hodsell. He ate paper."

"He ... ate ... paper," he said, staring at Ruby.

"Absolutely, Inspector," said Fina, as an instant rush of relief flooded her body. What a brilliant yet true excuse. "You can ask anyone who knew James. I remember that's the first thing I noticed about him in lecture one day. We sat in a packed room where I saw this young man casually tearing bits of paper and eating them. Perhaps it was a response to strain – or perhaps it was simply a habit. Either way, it explains the jagged paper."

"I see," he said, clearly not buying the explanation for a minute.

"You can confirm it with Mr Hayford – or wire someone in England to ask," said Ruby. She opened her handbag and drew out her wallet. She handed the inspector a card.

"Dean Primrose Ossington, Quenby College, Oxford," he read aloud in an impressed voice.

"Yes, Inspector. If you doubt our story, please contact Dean Ossington, and I'm sure she'll confirm our story about his paper-eating habit."

Mollified, he said, "Let's discuss why Mr Matua was on the train with you two – including Mr Hayford. I understand from Mr Hayford that you three were travelling in Sardinia, then Milan and then Genoa before taking the *Train Blanc.*"

"That's correct, Inspector. I'm a fashion designer, and Fina is my assistant. We were invited to a private weekend party of a famous shoe designer in Sardinia."

"And why was Mr Hayford with you at this weekend party?"

"Hasn't he already told you?" asked Ruby.

"Please just answer the question, Miss Dove," he said as he rotated his hat on the table.

"Well," she said, smoothing her hair. "He is a journalist friend of ours. When I told our host, Mr Carnevali, about him, he said it would be excellent publicity to have a journalist write about our possible new fashion collaboration. So he invited Mr Hayford to join us that weekend."

Scribble, scribble. Silence.

"Now let's get to the heart of the matter, shall we?"

"Let's, Inspector," said Fina. She couldn't help herself. Ruby shot her a warning look.

The inspector ignored or didn't perceive Fina's sarcasm. "Why was Mr Matua following you from Oxford to Sardinia to the *Train Blanc*?"

"Shall you tell him or shall I, Fina?" asked Ruby. Her face clearly indicated that Fina should be quiet.

"Oh no, please, you tell him."

"I'm afraid Fina is a bit embarrassed about this," said Ruby. As soon as the words 'Fina is a bit embarrassed' left Ruby's mouth, little pinpricks of warmth crept up Fina's neck.

"I can see she is," said the inspector, finally producing the ghost of a human smile.

"Yes. Well. We women are accustomed to men paying us unwanted attention." Fina almost burst out laughing at the use of the phrase 'unwanted attention'. "But to have a young man follow you halfway across the continent is not only embarrassing but somewhat alarming."

"We kept hoping he would go away but as one of us said upon boarding the *Train Blanc*, he kept turning up like a bad penny," said Fina.

"Did he harass you in any way, Miss Aubrey-Havelock?" asked the inspector with growing patriarchal protective alarm.

"No, no, Inspector. Not like that. At first, he was like a cute limpet, but soon became a leech."

"How so? I've never thought of a limpet as 'cute' before."

Fina shifted in her seat. "His behaviour was endearing at first, but when someone turns up everywhere you go – including out of the country – it becomes rather unnerving."

"Yes, I can see that. But he must have had a good

reason to be following you. Not to mention he must have had ample funds," he said, looking at Ruby rather than Fina.

"You're the inspector, Inspector," said Ruby. "You have more access to information than we do."

"That I do, Miss Dove," he said, sighing. Clearly, this interview was not going the way he'd planned. "So you can tell me nothing more about his suicide, other than what you know about the note and his disappearance."

"That's correct, Inspector," said Ruby.

Inspector Hodsell leapt up from his seat as if he had suddenly remembered a missed appointment. "Thank you for your time, ladies," he said, turning toward the door.

Then he turned his head over his shoulder. "Mind you, we'll still be keeping an eye on you two. I don't know why, but people more important than a lowly police inspector will be watching you."

35

"Brioche, please," said Fina as she sipped her café crème.

Ruby grinned at Fina. "Would you like a bit of my apple bostock? It's delicious."

"Don't mind if I do," said Fina, scooping up the sticky mess and thrusting it into her mouth. "You're right about that."

"Espresso for me, thank you," said Ian to the waiter, lighting a cigarette.

Fina absorbed the scenery of the quiet plaza. An elderly couple held hands in one corner, while a young couple nattered and quarrelled in another. Pigeons moved in waves across the square as a woman sprinkled food for them from a bench. The sky was blue and clear, and the day was sunny. Fina shivered. They had decided to sit outside even though it was November. Just for a bit and then they might pop back into the cafe if it became too cold. Ian agreed that food, coffee and cigarettes all tasted better in the fresh air. It hadn't taken long for him to find them after they had left the police station.

"So what kind of story are you going to salvage from our little adventure?" Ian asked, waving in Pixley's direction.

Pixley pulled his seat closer to the table and leaned over with a conspiratorial air. "I thought I'd write about the salacious life of an erotic author," he said in all seriousness.

"You must be joking. That's not your kind of news story, Pixley," said Ruby.

"Aha! Someone took the proverbial bait!" he said, bursting into a fit of giggles.

Ruby rolled her eyes.

"No, really, I can't figure out what to write without breaking a code of silence," he said, adjusting his spectacles as he jiggled his leg. "Any ideas? It's to your benefit I don't inadvertently reveal a secret."

"That's extortion, old man," said Ian.

Pixley grinned. "That's not fair. It's just part of my job. Now," he said, pencil hovering over his notebook.

"I suppose you could write about the life and times of Sophia Salazar," said Ian.

"Yes," said Pixley. "But to be honest, this drama has already made her a bit of a legend. And booksellers cannot keep enough copies on the shelf."

"In the rush to leave the train – and then the interminable interviews with Swiss police – I never found out what happened to the other passengers," said Fina. "Do any of you know?"

"I saw Father Schweinsteiger walk away from the police station when we were leaving," said Pixley. "I assume everything turned out for him since he was whistling a happy tune. Though I doubt he can stay two steps in front of his creditors much longer."

"Ada Hartman made a special effort to see me when she left the station," said Ruby, rubbing her arms in the chill. "She had those police officers eating out of her hand!" she laughed. "They were running around making cups of coffee for her and bringing a steady stream of sandwiches. They kept telling her how apologetic they were about having to hold her at the station."

"The Synges – or the family formerly known as Synge," said Pixley, sipping his espresso, "sailed through the police station within a matter of minutes. They must have been on the same diplomatic list as Mr Durand."

Something was niggling in the back of Fina's mind. Some loose end. She held up a finger in triumph. "Speaking of the Synges, did we ever clear up that business of Ridgewell's missing sketches? Or was that a completely unrelated incident?"

Pixley pushed his glasses up on his nose. "Ah, yes. I meant to tell you both about that but, in the confusion, it slipped my mind. I had suspicions that it was Dot who had made off with the sketches. It was just something about her demeanour that night when we first learned of Ridgewell's artistic talents. I confronted her about it and she crumbled quite easily. Must have been a guilty conscience."

"Well?" said Ruby, tapping her fingers on the table.

"It turns out it had nothing to do with much of anything. Turns out Dot is quite vain. She thought Ridgewell's sketches of her made her look old and haggard. So she tore them up – along with a few others for good measure. And to cover her tracks," said Pixley. He cleared his throat. "To return to your first question about what happened to the rest of the passengers, Mr Wistow also had a relatively easy time of it. The authorities held him a little longer than the Synges, but I heard an officer apologise as soon as they confirmed he was a former British colonial governor."

"And speaking of Mr Wistow," said Fina, looking at Ian. "Why did you want to speak to him when you were still hiding out in the front of the train?"

Ian tapped his espresso spoon against the cup meditatively. "Ah, yes, I thought I'd eventually have to tell you about that," he said, setting down the spoon and crossing his arms. "I had a little business with the former governor about his still-great influence over what happens in the Caribbean. Specifically, in St Kitts. Fortunately, he saw that it was in his best interests to cooperate."

"Let me guess. This is about the plantation uprisings," said Fina.

"Mmhhh," Ian affirmed.

"But how did you get him to cooperate?" asked Ruby.

"I said one word – *Eulalie*."

"Eulalie?" queried Ruby and Fina together.

"Yes, it worked like a charm." He paused. "I guess there's no reason not to tell you what it means. You see, Mr Wistow has certain proclivities that are not appreciated by the current government. Or probably any government, for that matter."

"I enjoy hearing about proclivities of any kind," Pixley chuckled.

"So do I!" said Fina with a little too much enthusiasm.

Ian smiled. "Eulalie is the name of a private club. It's not necessarily a physical club with a specific location, but more of an affinity group – if you can call it that. Wistow is the founder and organiser. It's completely harmless, of course, but it won't be seen that way if the press gets a hold of it." Ian took a sip of his espresso. He was clearly enjoying prolonging this revelation as long as possible. "The club meets in wealthy people's houses to engage in a bit of ... discipline."

Fina cocked her head. "You mean they tell each other off?"

"Not quite," chuckled Ian. "I mean they indulge in what you might call, to put it bluntly, spanking."

"No!" said Fina, scandalised.

Everyone burst out laughing. Fina joined in. After the laughing had subsided, she hurried to change the subject. "What about Raoul?"

Ruby shook her head.

Pixley polished his spectacles. "Mr Lapointe, or I should say, the man we know as Mr Lapointe, was the person of greatest interest to the police."

"Scarcely surprising, given his attachment to Sophia," said Fina. "So is he in jail?"

"I decided to intervene on that little matter," he said, flipping his fork over and over.

Ruby, Fina, and Ian all turned to stare at him. "Intervene?" queried Ian, his eyebrows wiggling.

Pixley cleared his throat. "Let's just say I told the Swiss police I could make this affair embarrassing for them if they decided to charge Raoul."

"Wait a moment. What would they charge him with, anyway?" asked Fina.

"Probably as an accessory to the crime," said Ruby.

Pixley nodded. "Well, we were certain that while he was rather furtive – for a good reason – he didn't assist Sophia in committing those crimes. Besides, even though I'm not that fond of cats, who would take care of little Ricki?"

Ruby giggled. "You are the simply the limit, my friend."

"So what did you do?" asked Ian.

"I told them I could embarrass them with an international story about this case. The problem was, they didn't believe I was a journalist, naturally. But once I had produced enough identification to satisfy them, they hemmed and hawed for about fifteen minutes. And then, presto! Raoul was free."

"With Ricki, of course," smiled Fina.

"Of course!"

Pixley tapped his fingers on the table.

"What are you keeping from us, Mr Hayford?" asked Ruby. "I know that look."

"Well..."

"Out with it, old man," said Ian. "Or I'll withhold that piece of tart that I see heading toward our table."

"That's hitting below the belt, Ian," said Pixley, licking his lips as the waiter set a gorgeous tart in front of him.

After the first bite, he said, "It has to do with Ricki. Remember how he had an odd collar?"

Fina stared into the sky. "Yes. I do. It was ornate and very heavy. It was more like a locket on a necklace."

"Mhhh..." he affirmed while chewing another piece of tart. "There was a good reason for it," he said, reaching into his pocket.

A green stone, the size of a small pebble, sparkled in the sunlight.

"Is that an emerald?" asked Ruby, nearly choking on her coffee.

"It most certainly is," he said, watching Ruby roll it around in her palm.

She looked up at him. "You're saying this was in Ricki's collar?"

"Yes. Raoul was so grateful for what I did to help him out of jail that he gave it to me. It represents his entire life's savings, I believe. The poor fellow was so petrified by the clampdown in Spain that he wasn't willing to leave anything behind. Do you know, I have a feeling that when Sophia told him they'd be travelling to Paris, Raoul bought a one-way ticket..." Pixley chewed meditatively on his pastry. "In any case, he'll take good care of Ricki. I tried to refuse the jewel at least ten times, but he said he knew I would put it to good use."

"We will," said Ruby. "We'll be sending that back to St Kitts – or at least the proceeds."

"All's well that ends well," said Ian, smiling.

"Hear, hear," mumbled Pixley, scraping his plate one more time.

They sat in silence for a few moments, soaking up the sun and finishing their coffee.

"I've had an idea," said Fina, taking a thoughtful sip of her café crème. "It's in answer to your original question, Pixley. What if you profiled the life of Neeya Arafa? She was extraordinary – it would be a fitting tribute."

"Excellent idea, Feens," said Ruby, snatching a piece of Ian's pain au chocolat.

Fina watched as Ian moved his seat an inch closer to

Ruby's. But she wasn't having it. Ruby's body posture signalled she was still furious with Ian about surprising her on the train. At least they were all sitting together in this lovely cafe.

Pixley cleared his throat. "I'll be travelling back to London tomorrow. And the rest of you?"

Ian glanced at Ruby. "I'll be—"

"Fina and I will be travelling with you tomorrow, Pixley," she said before Ian could finish his sentence. Ruby's pride couldn't let him say he'd be leaving them first.

Ian shifted in his seat and blew a perfect ring of smoke toward the blue sky. "I was about to say I would join you all on your journey home. I have business to attend to in London before I'm certain of my next destination."

The tiniest smile played across Ruby's mouth.

The End

If you enjoyed this book, would you leave a review on your favorite platform? Thank you!

SPECIAL THANKS TO READERS

Over the course of writing these five books, I've been so fortunate to have amazing Advance Reader Teams who've provided encouragement, feedback, and reviews that made me cry (tears of gratitude!). Here they are: Andrea, Anne, Beverley, Brent, Carol, Caroline, Cat, Charlene, Connie, Crystal, David, Dawn, Deb, Debbie, Derek, Diana, Diana, DJ, Dorothy, Elaine, Elena, Emmy, Fran, Ginny, Glenis, Grace, Heather, Ingrid, James, Jan, Janet, Jen, Joan, Joanna, Judy, Julia, Julie, Karen, Kate, Kathleen, Kerri, Lisa, Louise, Lyn, Mae, Mara, Margaret, Marianne, Mary, Mary Beth, MB, Michelle, Morgan, Nancy, Pamela, Pat, Patsy, Peggy, Pete, Rennee, Richard, Robbie, Robin, Roseanne, Rosemary, Sandra, Santosh, Sharon, Sheryl, Shirley, Sierra, Sudha, Sue, Susan, Teresa, Terry, Tina, Tracy, Umut, Wanda, and Yvonne.

Your kindness and generosity keeps me on track, especially on hard writing days. Thank you.

ENJOYED RUBY'S TRACKS?

I'm looking to you, dear reader, to share your views about this series. Reviews online are wonderful and word of mouth is even better.

If you enjoyed this book, I would be grateful if you spent a few minutes leaving me a review on your favorite book-reading platform.

The Ruby Dove Mystery Series:
The Mystery of Ruby's Sugar
The Mystery of Ruby's Port
The Mystery of Ruby's Smoke
Box Set: Mysteries 1-3
The Mystery of Ruby's Stiletto
The Mystery of Ruby's Tracks

Thank you!

ABOUT THE AUTHOR

Rose Donovan is a lifelong devotee of cozy (or cosy) mysteries. *The Ruby Dove Mystery Series* is her first foray into fiction, though she has written numerous non-fiction articles unraveling the mysteries of politics and injustice.

www.rosedonovan.com
rose@rosedonovan.com

NOTE ABOUT BRITISH STYLE

Readers fluent in US English may believe words such as "fuelled", "signalled", "hiccough", "fulfil", titbit", "oesophagus", "blinkers", and "practise" are typographical errors in this text. Rest assured this is simply British spelling. There are also other formatting differences in terms of spacing and punctuation, including periods after quotation marks in certain circumstances. I certainly learned a lot when making sure the prose was accurate!

For Dad

9 781950 203154